# SELECTED NOBEL LAUREATES' PRIZE ACCEPTANCE SPEECHES

**WITH BIOGRAPHICAL SKETCH**

## PHYSICS

## MEDICINE

## CHEMISTRY

Dr. Gagan Jain, D.Litt.

MG BOOKS
NEW DELHI (INDIA)

# SELECTED NOBEL LAUREATES' PRIZE ACCEPTANCE SPEECHES

WITH BIOGRAPHICAL SKETCH



*Published by*

MG BOOKS

*An Imprint of*

MAANU GRAPHICS

**MAANU GRAPHICS**

(PUBLISHERS OF GENERAL BOOKS)

5FF, Ganpati Bhawan, 21 Ansari Road,
Darya Ganj, New Delhi-110002
Ph: 65285220, 64138266
E-mail : maanugraphics@yahoo.com
mgbooks.maanu@yahoo.com



*Printed at*
Satyam Enterprises, Delhi

## CONTENTS

### PHYSICS

**MEDICINE**



**CHEMISTRY**

# PHYSICS

## GUGLIELMO MARCONI
## 1909

### INTRODUCTION

Guglielmo Marconi was born at Bologna, Italy, on April 25, 1874. He was educated privately at Bologna, Florence and Leghorn. In 1895 he began laboratory experiments at his father's country estate at Pontecchio where he succeeded in sending wireless signals over a distance of one and a half miles.

In 1899 he established wireless communication between France and England across the English Channel. He erected permanent wireless stations at The Needles, Isle of Wight, at Bournemouth and later at the Haven Hotel, Poole, Dorset.

In 1914 he was commissioned in the Italian Army as a Lieutenant being later promoted to Captain, and in 1916 transferred to the Navy in the rank of Commander. He was a member of the Italian Government mission to the United States in 1917 and in 1919 was appointed Italian plenipotentiary delegate to the Paris Peace Conference. He was awarded the Italian Military Medal in 1919 in recognition of his war service.

In 1931 Marconi began research into the propagation characteristics of still shorter waves, resulting in the opening in 1932 of the world's first microwave radiotelephone link between the Vatican City and the Pope's summer residence at Castel Gandolfo.

He has been the recipient of honorary doctorates of several universities and many other international honours and awards, among them the Nobel Prize for Physics, which in 1909 he shared with Professor Karl Braun, the Albert Medal of the Royal Society of Arts, the John Fritz Medal and the Kelvin Medal. He was decorated by the Tsar of Russia with the Order of St. Anne, the King of Italy created him Commander of the Order of St. Maurice and St. Lazarus, and awarded him the Grand Cross of the Order of the Crown of Italy in 1902. Marconi also received the freedom of the City of Rome (1903), and was created Chevalier of the Civil Order of Savoy in 1905. Many other distinctions of this kind followed. In 1914 he was both created a Senatore in the Italian Senate and app ointed Honorary Knight Grand Cross of the Royal Victorian Order in England. He received the hereditary title of Marchese in 1929. In 1905 he married the Hon.

Marconi died in Rome on July 20, 1937.

## PRIZE ACCEPTANCE SPEECH

*Guglielmo Marconi's speech at the Nobel Banquet in Stockholm, December 10, 1909*

*Your Royal Highnesses,*

*Your Excellencies, Ladies and Gentlemen*

I thank Mr. Hildebrand for the very kind but too flattering remarks that he has made of myself and of my work in Wireless Telegraphy.

I believe that one perhaps of the least thought of advantages enjoyed by the winner of the Nobel Prize is that he is asked to visit Sweden and thereby given an opportunity of appreciating the illustrious count of Linné, Schéele, Berzelius, and Arrhenius.

Thanks to the high standing which science has for so long attain and to the impartiality of the Nobel Prize Committee, the Nobel Prize for Physics is rightly considered everywhere as the highest reward within the reach of workers in that branch of Natural Philosophy.

I am also glad to have this opportunity of expressing my

high appreciation of the honour extended to me many years ago by the Royal Swedish Academy of Science by enrolling me amongst its members. You will also allow me to thank the Academy for inviting me to lecture in Stockholm, for its hospitality, and for the opportunity afforded me for admiring the charm of your people and the beauty of your country.

Your Royal Highnesses, Your Excellencies. Ladies and Gentlemen, I have the honour to ask you to drink to the health of Sweden and to the continued happiness and prosperity of the Swedish nation.

# CHARLES GLOVER BARKLA
## 1917

### INTRODUCTION

Charles Glover Barkla was born on June 7, 1877 at Widnes, Lancashire, England, where his father, J.M. Barkla, was Secretary to the Atlas Chemical Company. He was educated at the Liverpool Institute and entered University College, Liverpool, in 1894 to study mathematics and physics, the latter under Oliver Lodge. He graduated with First Class Honours in Physics in 1898 and in the following year he obtained his master's degree. Also in 1899, he was awarded a research scholarship by the Royal Commissioners for the Exhibition of 1851 and he proceeded to Trinity College, Cambridge, to work in the Cavendish Laboratory with J. J. Thomson. He migrated to King's College during 1900 and in 1902 returned to Liverpool as Oliver Lodge Fellow. From 1905 to 1909 he was successively demonstrator, assistant lecturer in physics and special lecturer in advanced electricity at the University, and in 1909 he succeeded H. A. Wilson as Wheatstone Professor of Physics in the University of London. In 1913, Barkla accepted the Chair in Natural Philosophy in the University of Edinburgh and he held this position until his death.

Barkla's first researches concerned the velocity of electric waves along wires but in 1902 he commenced his investigations on Röntgen radiation which were to occupy almost his whole life. His discovery of homogeneous radiations characteristic of the elements showed that these elements had their characteristic line spectra in X-ray and he was the first to show that secondary emission is of two kinds, one consisting of X-rays scattered unchanged, and the other a fluorescent radiation peculiar to the particular substance. He discovered the polarisation of X-rays, an experimental result of considerable importance for it meant that X-radiation could be regarded as similar to ordinary light. Barkla made valuable contributions to present knowledge on the absorption and photographic action of X-rays and his later work demonstrated the relation between the characteristic X-radiation and the corpuscular radiation accompanying it. He has also shown both the applicability and the limitation of the quantum theory in relation to Röntgen radiation. The results of his findings are recorded in various papers which have appeared mainly in the Transactions and Proceedings of the Royal Society. He had a considerable reputation as an examiner in physics.

Barkla, a Fellow of the Royal Society, had several honorary degrees. He was appointed Bakerian Lecturer (Royal Society) in 1916 and he was awarded the Hughes Medal in the following year.

Barkla died at his home, Braidwood, Edinburgh, on October 23, 1944.

## PRIZE ACCEPTANCE SPEECH

*Charles Glover Barkla's speech at the Nobel Banquet in Stockholm, June 1, 1920*

Let me first say how much I regret that the British are not more fully represented at this celebration. When the invitation came to hand Professor Sir W.H. Bragg had already entered into several important engagements which could not conveniently be cancelled, and unfortunately Professor W.L. Bragg did not receive his invitation until too late to make preparations for the journey.

The Nobel Prize is without doubt the highest honour, the most coveted honour, which can be bestowed on a Scientist. There are of course very obvious reasons for this. It would be affectation on my part not to mention the monetary value of the prize; this is especially important at the present time, when rewards are given more than ever to those who can show the immediate practical results of their labours, and when those who seek knowledge and search after new methods are in danger of being left to pursue their course unrecognised and unheeded. Not only is the reward of great assistance to the scientist whose remuneration is slight; it impresses on 'the man in the street' as nothing else could, the importance of work being accomplished in a sphere far removed from his own. Further, the majority of honours are awarded with a definite and intentional bias in favour of scientists of certain nationality, whereas the Nobel awards are made without consideration either of social position or of nationality. Let me say what a unique position the Swedish Academy of Science holds among all the scientific societies of the world. It has the power such as no other body possesses, to put its stamp, - its hall-mark - upon the work of any investigator, indeed to put the stamp upon any man or woman and to mark him or her out as a person of undisputed eminence, a person whose name shall endure. This is a position of great responsibility. May I congratulate the Swedish Academy of Science on the impartiality which it has hitherto shown in its selections. The Nobel Prize is a truly international award.

So remarkable is this that even in Edinburgh people have asked if Barkla must not be a Swede, that he should receive this recognition in Sweden. Perhaps there is some excuse for this question in what appears to be the Scandinavian form of the name Barkla. I am afraid, however, I can't claim the possession of Swedish blood.

As an Englishman permit me now to say with what pleasure I learnt of the election of Professor Planck and Professor Stark to the Nobel Prizes for the years 1918 and 1919. I mention these because they have been most recently announced, and because the work for which the awards were made, being in my own particular field of science, is familiar to me. Planck's theory of radiation and Planck's constant are on every physicist's lips. Indeed it is impossible to deliver courses of lectures to university students without repeated reference to Planck's investigations. My relations with Professor Stark have been of a somewhat more personal nature. I think I can truly say that I owe almost as much to Professor Stark as to any man for the publicity given to my own work on Rontgen radiation. For it was at Professor Starck's invitation that I gave in the Jahrbuch der Radioaktivitat und Elektronik the first full and connected account of my investigations on Secondary Radiations. I am glad that Professor Stark's numerous and meritorious investigations have received the recognition which was their due.

I am happy to meet these distinguished Germans in this city so renowned for its hospitality. It is a privilege to visit such a city, to see its palatial buildings devoted to the study of science, and to meet its world-famous scientists - of whom I may specially mention Professor Arrhenius.

It seems to me that the Swedish Academy of Science may be qualifying for the Nobel Peace Prize. It recognises no nationality; it discourages unworthy national feeling and prejudice. We are all dwellers on this one small earth; we live one life, die one death; we have the same difficulties to contend with; we ought in common to fight the foes of ignorance and wrong.

I thank you again for your great kindness, and for a real Swedish welcome.

# ALBERT EINSTEIN
## 1921

### INTRODUCTION

Albert Einstein was born at Ulm, in Württemberg, Germany, on March 14, 1879. Six weeks later the family moved to Munich, where he later on began his schooling at the Luitpold Gymnasium. Later, they moved to Italy and Albert continued his education at Aarau, Switzerland and in 1896 he entered the Swiss Federal Polytechnic School in Zurich to be trained as a teacher in physics and mathematics. In 1901, the year he gained his diploma, he acquired Swiss citizenship and, as he was unable to find a teaching post, he accepted a position as technical assistant in the Swiss Patent Office. In 1905 he obtained his doctor's degree.

He became a German citizen in 1914 and remained in Berlin until 1933 when he renounced his citizenship for political reasons and emigrated to America to take the position of Professor of Theoretical Physics at Princeton.

Einstein always appeared to have a clear view of the problems of physics and the determination to solve them. He had a strategy of his own and was able to visualize the main stages on the way to his goal. He regarded his major achievements as mere stepping-stones for the next advance.

At the start of his scientific work, Einstein realized the inadequacies of Newtonian mechanics and his special theory of relativity stemmed from an attempt to reconcile the laws of mechanics with the laws of the electromagnetic field. He dealt with classical problems of statistical mechanics and problems in which they were merged with quantum theory: this led to an explanation of the Brownian movement of molecules. He investigated the thermal properties of light with a low radiation density and his observations laid the foundation of the photon theory of light.

In the 1920's, Einstein embarked on the construction of unified field theories, although he continued to work on the probabilistic interpretation of quantum theory, and he persevered with this work in America. After his retirement he continued to work towards the unification of the basic concepts of physics, taking the opposite approach, geometrisation, to the majority of physicists.

Einstein's researches are, of course, well chronicled and his more important works include *Special Theory of Relativity* (1905), *Relativity* (English translations, 1920 and 1950), *General Theory of Relativity* (1916), *Investigations on Theory of Brownian Movement* (1926), and *The Evolution of Physics* (1938). Among his non-scientific works, *About Zionism* (1930), *Why War?* (1933), *My Philosophy* (1934), and *Out of My Later Years* (1950) are perhaps the most important.

Albert Einstein received honorary doctorate degrees in science, medicine and philosophy from many European and American universities. During the 1920's he lectured in Europe, America and the Far East and he was awarded Fellowships or Memberships of all the leading scientific academies throughout the world. He gained numerous awards in recognition of his work, including the Copley Medal of the Royal Society of London in 1925, and the Franklin Medal of the Franklin Institute in 1935.

Einstein's gifts inevitably resulted in his dwelling much in intellectual solitude and, for relaxation, music played an important part in his life. He married Mileva Maric in 1903 and they had a daughter and two sons; their marriage was dissolved in 1919 and in the same year he married his cousin, Elsa Löwenthal, who died in 1936. He died on April 18, 1955 at Princeton, New Jersey.

## PRIZE ACCEPTANCE SPEECH

*Lecture delivered to the Nordic Assembly of Naturalists at Gothenburg (The Lecture was not delivered on the occasion of the Nobel Prize award, and did not, therefore, concern the discovery of the photoelectric effect.)*

*Lecture, July 11, 1923*

## Fundamental ideas and problems of the theory of relativity

If we consider that part of the theory of relativity which may nowadays in a sense be regarded as bona fide scientific knowledge, we note two aspects which have a major bearing on this theory. The whole development of the theory turns on the question of whether there are physically preferred states of motion in Nature (physical relativity problem). Also, concepts and distinctions are only admissible to the extent that observable facts can be assigned to them without ambiguity (stipulation that concepts and distinctions should have meaning). This postulate, pertaining to epistemology, proves to be of fundamental importance. These two aspects become clear when applied to a special case, e.g. to classical mechanics. Firstly we see that at any point filled with matter there exists a preferred state of motion, namely that of the substance at the point considered. Our problem starts however with the question whether physically preferred states of motion exist in reference to *extensive* regions. From the viewpoint of classical mechanics the answer is in the affirmative; the physically preferred states of motion from the viewpoint of mechanics are those of the inertial frames.

This assertion, in common with the basis of the whole of mechanics as it generally used to be described before the relativity theory, far from meets the above "stipulation of meaning". Motion can only be conceived as the relative motion of bodies. In mechanics, motion relative to the system of coordinates is implied when merely motion is referred to. Nevertheless this interpretation does not comply with the "stipulation of meaning" if the coordinate system is considered as something purely imaginary. If we turn our attention to experimental physics we see that there the coordinate system is invariably represented by a "practically rigid" body. Furthermore it is assumed that such rigid bodies can be positioned in rest relative to one another in common with the bodies of Euclidian geometry.

Insofar as we may think of the rigid measuring body as existing as an object which can be experienced, the "system of coordinates" concept as well as the concept of the motion of matter relative thereto can be accepted in the sense of the "stipulation of meaning". At the same time Euclidian geometry, by this conception, has been adapted to the requirements of the physics of the "stipulation of meaning".

The question whether Euclidian geometry is valid becomes physically significant; its validity is assumed in classical physics and also later in the special theory of relativity. In classical mechanics the inertial frame and time are best defined together by a suitable formulation of the law of inertia: It is possible to fix the time and assign a state of motion to the system of coordinates (inertial frame) such that, with reference to the latter, force-free material points undergo no acceleration; furthermore it is assumed that this time can be measured without disagreement by identical clocks (systems which run down periodically) in any arbitrary state of m*Lecture delivered to the Nordic Assembly of Naturalists at Gothenburg*otion. There are then an infinite number of inertial frames which are in uniform translational motion relative to each other, and hence there is also an infinite number of mutually equivalent, physically preferred states of motion. Time is absolute, i.e.independent of the choice of the particular inertial frame; it is defined by more characteristics than logically necessary, although - as implied by mechanics - this should not lead to contradictions with experience. Note in passing that the logical weakness of this exposition from the point of view of the stipulation of meaning is the lack of an experimental criterion for whether a material point is forcefree or not; therefore the concept of the inertial frame remains rather problematical. This deficiency leads to the general theory of relativity. We shall not consider it for the moment.

The concept of the rigid body (and that of the clock) has a key bearing on the foregoing consideration of the fundamentals of mechanics, a bearing which there is some justification for challenging. The rigid body is only approximately achieved in Nature, not even with desired approximation; this concept does not therefore strictly satisfy the "stipulation of meaning". It is also logically unjustifiable to base all physical consideration on the rigid or solid body and then finally reconstruct that body atomically by means of elementary physical laws which in turn have been determined by means of the rigid measuring body. I am mentioning these deficiencies of method because in the same sense they are also a feature of the relativity theory in the schematic exposition which I am advocating here. Certainly it would be logically more correct to begin with the whole of the laws and to apply the "stipulation of meaning" to this whole first, i.e. to put the unambiguous relation to the world of experience last instead of already fulfilling it in an imperfect form for an artificially isolated part, namely the space-time metric. We are not, however, sufficiently advanced in our knowledge of Nature's elementary laws to adopt this more perfect method without going out of our depth. At the close of our considerations we shall see that in the most recent studies there is an attempt, based on ideas by Levi-Civita, Weyl, and Eddington, to implement that logically purer method. It more clearly follows from the above what is implied by "preferred states of motion". They are preferred as regards the laws of Nature. States of motion are preferred when, relative to the formulation of the laws of Nature, coordinate systems within them are distinguished in that with respect to them those laws assume a form preferred by simplicity. According to classical mechanics the states of motion of the inertial frames in this sense are physically preferred. Classical mechanics permits a distinction to be made between (absolutely) unaccelerated and accelerated motions; it also claims that velocities have only a relative existence (dependent on the selection of the inertial frame), while accelerations and rotations have an absolute existence (independent of the selection of the inertial frame). This state of affairs can be expressed thus: According to classical mechanics "velocity relativity" exists, but not "acceleration relativity". After these preliminary considerations we can pass to the actual topic of our contemplations, the relativity theory, by characterizing its development so far in terms of principles. The special theory of relativity is an adaptation of physical principles to Maxwell-Lorentz electrodynamics. From earlier physics it takes the assumption that Euclidian geometry is valid for the laws governing the position of rigid bodies, the inertial frame and the law of inertia. The postulate of equivalence of inertial frames for the formulation of the laws of Nature is assumed to be valid for the whole of physics (special relativity principle). From Maxwell-Lorentz electrodynamics it takes the postulate of invariance of the velocity of light in a vacuum (light principle).

To harmonize the relativity principle with the light principle, the assumption that an absolute time (agreeing for all inertial frames) exists, had to be abandoned. Thus the hypothesis is abandoned that arbitrarily moved and suitably set identical clocks function in such a way that the times shown by two of them, which meet, agree. A specific time is assigned to each inertial frame; the state of motion and the time of the inertial frame are defined, in accordance with the stipulation of meaning, by the requirement that the light principle should apply to it. The existence of the inertial frame thus defined and the validity of the law of inertia with respect to it are assumed. The time for each inertial frame is measured by identical clocks that are stationary relative to the frame.

The laws of transformation for space coordinates and time for the transition from one inertial frame to another, the Lorentz transformations as they are termed, are unequivocally established by these definitions and the hypotheses concealed in the assumption that they are free from contradiction. Their immediate physical significance lies in the effect of the motion relative to the used inertial frame on the form of rigid bodies (Lorentz contraction) and on the rate of the clocks. According to the special relativity principle the laws of Nature must be covariant relative to Lorentz transformations; the theory thus provides a criterion for general laws of Nature. It leads in particular to a modification of the Newtonian point motion law in which the velocity of light in a vacuum is considered the limiting velocity, and it also leads to the realization that energy and inertial mass are of like nature. The special relativity theory resulted in appreciable advances.

It reconciled mechanics and electrodynamics. It reduced the number of logically independent hypotheses regarding the latter. It enforced the need for a clarification of the fundamental concepts in epistemological terms. It united the momentum and energy principle, and demonstrated the like nature of mass and energy. Yet it was not entirely satisfactory - quite apart from the quantum problems, which all theory so far has been incapable of really solving. In common with classical mechanics the special relativity theory favours certain states of motion - namely those of the inertial frames - to all other states of motion. This was actually more difficult to tolerate than the preference for a single state of motion as in the case of the theory of light with a stationary ether, for this imagined a real reason for the preference, i.e. the light ether. A theory which from the outset prefers no state of motion should appear more satisfactory. Moreover the previously mentioned vagueness in the definition of the inertial frame or in the formulation of the law of inertia raises doubts which obtain their decisive importance, owing to the empirical principle for the equality of the inertial and heavy mass, in the light of the following consideration.

Let K be an inertial frame without a gravitational field, K' a system of coordinates accelerated uniformly relative to K. The behaviour of material points relative to K' is the the same as if K' were an inertial frame in respect of which a homogeneous gravitational field exists. On the basis of the empirically known properties of the gravitational field, the definition of the inertial frame thus proves to be weak. The conclusion is obvious that any arbitrarily moved frame of reference is equivalent to any other for the formulation of the laws of Nature, that there are thus no physically preferred states of motion at all in respect of regions of finite extension (general relativity principle).

The implementation of this concept necessitates an even more profound modification of the geometric-kinematical principles than the special relativity theory. The Lorentz contraction, which is derived from the latter, leads to the conclusion that with regard to a system K' arbitrarily moved relative to a (gravity field free) inertial frame K, the laws of Euclidian geometry governing the position of rigid (at rest relative to K') bodies do not apply.

Consequently the Cartesian system of coordinates also loses its significance in terms of the stipulation of meaning. Analogous reasoning applies to time; with reference to K' the time can no longer meaningfully be defined by the indication on identical clocks at rest relative to K', nor by the law governing the propagation of light. Generalizing, we arrive at the conclusion that gravitational field and metric are only different manifestations of the same physical field. We arrive at the formal description of this field by the following consideration.

For each infinitesimal point-environment in an arbitrary gravitational field a local frame of coordinates can be given for such a state of motion that relative to this local frame no gravitational field exists (local inertial frame). In terms of this inertial frame we may regard the results of the special relativity theory as correct to a first approximation for this infinitesimally small region. There are an infinite number of such local inertial frames at any space-time point; they are associated by Lorentz transformations. These latter are characterised in that they leave invariant the "distance" ds of two infinitely adjacent point events - defined by the equation: &z = C2&Z - dxz _ dY2 _ dZ2 which distance can be measured by means of scales and clocks. For, *x, y, z, t* represent coordinates and time measured with reference to a local inertial frame.

To describe space-time regions of finite extent arbitrary point coordinates in four dimensions are required which serve no other purpose than to provide an unambiguous designation of the space-time points by four numbers each, *x1, x2, x3* and *x4,* which takes account of the continuity of this fourdimensional manifold (Gaussian coordinates). The mathematical expression of the general relativity principle is then, that the systems of equations expressing the general laws of Nature are equal for all such systems of coordinates. Since the coordinate differentials of the local inertial frame are expressed linearly by the differentials *dxv* of a Gaussian system of coordinates, when the latter is used, for the distance ds of two events an expression of the form ds2 = %w d-y+, kpv = gv,) is obtained. The *gm v* which arc continuous functions of *xv*, determine the metric in the four-dimensional manifold where ds is defined as an (absolute) parameter measurable by means of rigid scales and clocks. These same parameters *gm v* however also describe with reference to the Gaussian system of coordinates the gravitational field which we have previously found to be identical with the physical cause of the metric. The case as to the validity of the special relativity theory for finite regions is characterised in that when the system of coordinates is suitably chosen, the values of *gmv* for finite regions are independent of *xv*. In accordance with the general theory of relativity the law of point motion in the pure gravitational field is expressed by the equation for the geodetic line. Actually the geodetic line is the simplest mathematically which in the special case of constant *gm v* becomes rectilinear. Here therefore we are confronted with the transfer of Galileo's law of inertia to the general theory of relativity.

In mathematical terms the search for the field equations amounts to ascertaining the simplest generally covariant differential equations to which the gravitational potentials *gm v* can be subjected. By definition these equations should not contain higher derivatives of gm *v* with respect to xv than the second, and these only linearly, which condition reveals these equations to be a logical transfer of the Poisson field equation of the Newtonian theory of gravity to the general theory of relativity.

The considerations mentioned led to the theory of gravity which yields the Newtonian theory as a first approximation and furthermore it yields the motion of the perihelion of Mercury, the deflection of light by the sun, and the red shift of spectral lines in agreement with experience.(As regards the red shift, the agreement with experience is not yet completely assured, however.)

To complete the basis of the general theory of relativity, the electromagnetic field must still be introduced into it which, according to our present conviction, is also the material from which we must build up the elementary structures of matter. The Maxwellian field equations can readily be adopted into the general theory of relativity. This is a completely unambiguous adoption provided it is assumed that the equations contain no differential quotients of *gm v* higher than the first, and that in the customary Maxwellian form they apply in the local inertial frame. It is also easily possible to supplement the gravitational field equations by electromagnetic terms in a manner specified by the Maxwellian equations so that they contain the gravitational effect of the electromagnetic field.

These field equations have not provided a theory of matter. To incorporate the field generating effect of ponderable masses in the theory, matter had therefore (as in classical physics) to be introduced into the theory in an approximate, phenomenological representation.

And that exhausts the direct consequences of the relativity principle. I shall turn to those problems which are related to the development which I have traced. Already Newton recognized that the law of inertia is unsatisfactory in a context so far unmentioned in this exposition, namely that it gives no real cause for the special physical position of the states of motion of the inertial frames relative to all other states of motion. It makes the observable material bodies responsible for the gravitational behaviour of a material point, yet indicates no material cause for the inertial behaviour of the material point but devises the cause for it (absolute space or inertial ether). This is not logically inadmissible although it is unsatisfactory. For this reason E. Mach demanded a modification of the law of inertia in the sense that the inertia should be interpreted as an acceleration resistance of the bodies against *one another* and not against "space". This interpretation governs the expectation that accelerated bodies have concordant accelerating action in the same sense on other bodies (acceleration induction).

This interpretation is even more plausible according to general relativity which eliminates the distinction between inertial and gravitational effects. It amounts to stipulating that, apart from the arbitrariness governed by the free choice of coordinates, the *g*m *v* -field shall be completely determined by the matter. Mach's stipulation is favoured in general relativity by the circumstance that acceleration induction in accordance with the gravitational field equations really exists, although of such slight intensity that direct detection by mechanical experiments is out of the question.

Mach's stipulation can be accounted for in the general theory of relativity by regarding the world in spatial terms as finite and self-contained. This hypothesis also makes it possible to assume the mean density of matter in the world as finite, whereas in a spatially infinite (quasi-Euclidian) world it should disappear. It cannot, however, be concealed that to satisfy Mach's postulate in the manner referred to a term with no experimental basis whatsoever must be introduced into the field equations, which term logically is in no way determined by the other terms in the equations. For this reason this solution of the "cosmological problem" will not be completely satisfactory for the time being. A second problem which at present is the subject of lively interest is the identity between the gravitational field and the electromagnetic field. The mind striving after unification of the theory cannot be satisfied that two fields should exist which, by their nature, are quite independent. A mathematically unified field theory is sought in which the gravitational field and the electromagnetic field are interpreted only as different components or manifestations of the same uniform field, the field equations where possible no longer consisting of logically mutually independent summands. The gravitational theory, considered in terms of mathematical formalism, i.e. Riemannian geometry, should be generalized so that it includes the laws of the electromagnetic field. Unfortunately we are unable here to base ourselves on empirical facts as when deriving the gravitational theory (equality of the inertial and heavy mass), but we are restricted to the criterion of mathematical simplicity which is not free from arbitrariness. The attempt which at present appears the most successful is that, based on the ideas of Levi-Civita, Weyl and Eddington, to replace

Riemannian metric geometry by the more general theory of affine correlation.

The characteristic assumption of Riemannian geometry is the attribution to two infinitely adjacent points of a "distance" $ds$, the square of which is a homogeneous second order function of the coordinate differentials. It follows from this that (apart from certain conditions of reality) Euclidian geometry is valid in any infinitely small region. Hence to every line element (or vector) at a point P is assigned a parallel and equal line element (or vector) through any given infinitesimally adjacent point P' (affine correlation). Riemannian metric determines an affine correlation. Conversely, however, when an affine correlation (law of infinitesimal parallel displacement) is mathematically given, generally no Riemannian metric determination exists from which it can be derived.

The most important concept of Riemannian geometry, "space curvature", on which the gravitational equations are also based, is based exclusively on the "affine correlation". If one is given in a continuum, without first proceeding from a metric, it constitutes a generalization of Riemannian geometry but which still retains the most important derived parameters. By seeking the simplest differential equations which can be obeyed by an affine correlation there is reason to hope that a generalization of the gravitation equations will be found which includes the laws of the electromagnetic field.

This hope has in fact been fulfilled although I do not know whether the formal connection so derived can really be regarded as an enrichment of physics as long as it does not yield any new physical connections. In particular a field theory can, to my mind, only be satisfactory when it permits the elementary electrical bodies to be represented as solutions free from singularities. Moreover it should not be forgotten that a theory relating to the elementary electrical structures is inseparable from the quantum theory problems. So far also relativity theory has proved ineffectual in relation to this most profound physical problem of the present time. Should the form of the general equations some day, by the solution of the quantum problem, undergo a change however profound, even if there is a complete change in the parameters by means of which we represent the elementary process, the relativity principle will not be relinquished and the laws previously derived therefrom will at least retain their significance as limiting laws.

# NIELS BOHR
## 1922

### INTRODUCTION

Niels Henrik David Bohr was born in Copenhagen on October 7, 1885, as the son of Christian Bohr, Professor of Physiology at Copenhagen University, and his wife Ellen, *née* Adler.

After matriculation at the Gammelholm Grammar School in 1903, he entered Copenhagen University where he came under the guidance of Professor C. Christiansen, a profoundly original and highly endowed physicist, and took his Master's degree in Physics in 1909 and his Doctor's degree in 1911.

While still a student, the announcement by the Academy of Sciences in Copenhagen of a prize to be awarded for the solution of a certain scientific problem, caused him to take up an experimental and theoretical investigation of the surface tension by means of oscillating fluid jets. This work, which he carried out in his father's laboratory and for which he received the prize offered (a gold medal), was published in the Transactions of the Royal Society, 1908.

In the autumn of 1911 he made a stay at Cambridge, where he profited by following the experimental work going on in the Cavendish Laboratory under Sir J.J. Thomson's guidance, at the same time as he pursued own theoretical studies. In the spring of 1912 he was at work in Professor Rutherford's laboratory in Manchester, where just in those years such an intensive scientific life and activity prevailed as a consequence of that investigator's fundamental inquiries into the radioactive phenomena.

In 1913-1914 Bohr held a Lectureship in Physics at Copenhagen University and in 1914-1916 a similar appointment at the Victoria University in Manchester. In 1916 he was appointed Professor of Theoretical Physics at Copenhagen University, and since 1920 (until his death in 1962) he was at the head of the Institute for Theoretical Physics, established for him at that university. Recognition of his work on the structure of atoms came with the award of the Nobel Prize for 1922.

Among Professor Bohr's numerous writings (some 115 publications), three appearing as books in the English language may be mentioned here as embodying his principal thoughts: *The Theory of Spectra and Atomic Constitution*, University Press, Cambridge, 1922/2nd. ed., 1924; *Atomic Theory and the Description of Nature*, University Press, Cambridge, 1934/ reprint 1961; *The Unity of Knowledge*, Doubleday & Co., New York, 1955.

Professor Bohr was married, in 1912, to Margrethe Nørlund, who was for him an ideal companion.

Niels Bohr died in Copenhagen on November 18, 1962

## PRIZE ACCEPTANCE SPEECH

*Niels Bohr's speech at the Nobel Banquet in Stockholm, December 10, 1922*

*(Translation)*

*Your Royal Highnesses, Ladies and Gentlemen.*

In attempting to give expression to my deep and heartfelt gratitude for the great honour that the Royal Swedish Academy of Sciences has bestowed upon me by awarding me the Nobel Prize for Physics for this year, I am naturally forcibly reminded of Alfred Nobel's insistence upon the international character of science, which indeed forms the very basis of his most munificent bequest. That point of view - the international character of science - suggests itself all the more readily to myself, as the contributions that I may have had the good fortune to make to the development of physical science consist in a combination of the results arrived at by a number of fellow-investigators, belonging to a variety of nations, on the basis of study carried on under widely differing scientific traditions.

The grand discoveries which scientific experiment yielded at and about the turn of the century, in which investigators in many countries took an eminent part and which were destined all unexpectedly to give us a fresh insight into the structure of atoms, were due in the first instance, as all are aware, to the work of the great investigators of the English school, Sir Joseph Thomson and Sir Ernest Rutherford, who have inscribed their names on the tablets of the history of scientific research as distinguished witnesses to the truth that imagination and acumen are capable of penetrating the crowded mass of registered experience and of revealing Nature's simplicity to our gaze. On the other hand, abstract thinking, which throughout the ages has been one of the most powerful of man's aids in lifting the veil that shrouds the laws of Nature from the eyes of the uninitiated observer, has proved of the utmost importance for enabling the insight into the structure of atoms so obtained to be applied practically in elucidating the properties of those elements that are immediately accessible to our perceptions. To this branch of the work too, men of many nations have made important contributions; but it was the great German investigators, Planck and Einstein, who, as a result of their systematic abstract investigations, were to show us for the first time that the laws of the movements of atomic particles, which determine the properties of the elements, are of an essentially different character from those laws by the aid of which science has hitherto sought to bring order into the mass of our observations of natural phenomena. If it has been my good fortune to be in some sense a connecting link at one point in the development, that is but one among many evidences of the fruitfulness of the closest relations prevailing in the scientific world between those carrying on investigations under varying human conditions. A Danish scientist, however, on finding himself in Stockholm on such an occasion as this, cannot confine his thoughts to the international character of science but must also dwell in an equal degree on the intellectual solidarity that exists in these Scandinavian countries, of which we are all - and, especially in the domain of science - fully and perfectly aware. It might be tempting to endeavour to indicate the great debt owed by science, and consequently by Danish investigators, to Swedish scientists of earlier and recent times. That, however, would carry me too far, even if I were to confine myself only to the most important of the contributions that we owe to the distinguished representatives of Swedish investigations in natural science who are present here this evening, and whose work in a variety of ways has been of fundamental importance, for instance, for atomic research. Hence I must rest content only to recall the name of one single Swedish physicist, the late Professor Rydberg of Lund, whose brilliant work on the spectral laws has been of such great importance for extending our knowledge of atoms and especially for the particular contribution that it was to fall to my lot to make.

In once more gladly availing myself of this opportunity to express my deep gratitude for the honour that the Academy of Sciences has bestowed upon myself and upon Danish scientific investigation by awarding me the Nobel Prize, I also beg leave at this banquet to propose the toast of International Cooperation for the Advancement of Science, which is, I may say, in these so manifoldly depressing times, one of the bright spots visible in human existence, and also to give you, in particular, Prosperity to the sense of unity and solidarity in scientific work among the peoples of Scandinavia who, notwithstanding the characteristic peculiarities of each, do feel themselves intimately bound together by the ties of racial affinity.

# ARTHUR H. COMPTON
# 1927

## INTRODUCTION

Arthur Holly Compton was born at Wooster, Ohio, on September 10th, 1892, the son of Elias Compton, Professor of Philosophy and Dean of the College of Wooster. He was educated at the College, graduating Bachelor of Science in 1913, and he spent three years in postgraduate study at Princeton University receiving his M.A. degree in 1914 and his Ph.D. in 1916. After spending a year as instructor of physics at the University of Minnesota, he took a position as a research engineer with the Westinghouse Lamp Company at Pittsburgh until 1919 when he studied at Cambridge University as a National Research Council Fellow. In 1920, he was appointed Wayman Crow Professor of Physics, and Head of the Department of Physics at the Washington University, St. Louis; and in 1923 he moved to the University of Chicago as Professor of Physics. Compton returned to St. Louis as Chancellor in 1945 and from 1954 until his retirement in 1961 he was Distinguished Service Professor of Natural Philosophy at the Washington University.

In his early days at Princeton, Compton devised an elegant method for demonstrating the Earth's rotation, but he was soon to begin his studies in the field of X-rays. He developed a theory of the intensity of X-ray reflection from crystals as a means of studying the arrangement of electrons and atoms, and in 1918 he started a study of X-ray scattering.

During 1930-1940, Compton led a world-wide study of the geographic variations of the intensity of cosmic rays, thereby fully confirming the observations made in 1927 by J. Clay from Amsterdam of the influence of latitude on cosmic ray intensity.

Compton has numerous papers on scientific record and he is the author of *Secondary Radiations Produced by X-rays* (1922), *X-Rays and Electrons* (1926, second edition 1928), *X-Rays in Theory and Experiment* (with S. K. Allison, 1935, this being the revised edition of *X-rays and Electrons*), *The Freedom of Man* (1935, third edition 1939), *On Going to College* (with others, 1940), and *Human Meaning of Science* (1940).

Dr. Compton was awarded numerous honorary degrees and other distinctions including the Rumford Gold Medal (American Academy of Arts and Sciences), 1927; Gold Medal of Radiological Society of North America, 1928; Hughes Medal (Royal Society) and Franklin Medal (Franklin Institute), 1940.

He served as President of the American Physical Society (1934), of the American Association of Scientific Workers (1939-1940), and of the American Association for the Advancement of Science (1942).

In 1941 Compton was appointed Chairman of the National Academy of Sciences Committee to Evaluate Use of Atomic Energy in War. His investigations, carried out in cooperation with E. Fermi, L. Szilard, E. P. Wigner and others, led to the establishment of the first controlled uranium fission reactors, and, ultimately, to the large plutonium-producing reactors in Hanford, Washington, which produced the plutonium for the Nagasaki bomb, in August 1945.

Compton's chief recreations were tennis, astronomy, photography and music.

He died on March 15th, 1962, in Berkeley, California.

## PRIZE ACCEPTANCE SPEECH

*Arthur H. Compton's speech at the Nobel Banquet in Stockholm, December 10, 1927*

*Your Royal Highnesses, Ladies and Gentlemen:*

Several years ago I was reading Marco Polo's account of his experiences in the employ of the great Emperor of China,

Kublai Khan. He was telling his incredulous Venetian friends of the daily life of the Chinese. "They take two baths daily", he wrote, "one in the morning and another in the evening. Not only this, but the baths are in warm water". The idea of daily baths was itself sufficiently difficult for the Venetians to believe, but that water could be warmed twice daily seemed to them to present an insurmountable difficulty.

Polo replied that it would indeed have been impossible to heat the water for millions of Chinese if they had relied on wood for fuel. They had however solved the difficulty by finding a kind of black rock which would burn. This rock had the advantage over wood that it would hold its fire overnight and have the water warm for the morning bath. Then Polo described in accurate detail how this black rock occurred in veins in the mountains, and the manner in which it was quarried. If the idea of baths twice daily was marvelous, the story of the burning rocks was beyond the realm of possibility.

Marco Polo's stories read like the tales of a man who after visiting a highly civilized country returns to his semi-barbaric home to tell of the wonders he has seen. At that time, hardly seven centuries ago, China was far in advance of Italy, a land whose culture was the pride of our Western civilization.

Last year I had the privilege of visiting China, and I saw what, gauged by Western standards, was a primitive country. In seven short centuries the leadership has passed from the East to the West, until now we are as far ahead of the Orient as in Polo's day China was ahead of Italy.

Why this rapid change? Differences in native ability will not explain it. It was only a few centuries ago that a Mongolian ruler, Jenghis Khan, held sway over the greatest empire, with regard to both area and population, which has ever been united under one government. Nor have the Chinese been lacking in feats of engineering. The Great Wall of China, a massive pile of masonry extending over mountainous country for fifteen hundred miles, takes a high place among the wonders of the world. Is it doubtful whether either in individual ability or in aptitude for organization the European has any real advantage over the Mongolian.

Shortly after the days of Polo, however, there arose in various parts of Europe the scientific spirit - the eagerness to learn from Nature her truths, and to put these truths to the use of mankind. The rapid change in our mode of living since that time can certainly be traced to the consequences of the development of this spirit of science. When we seek the reason for the present preeminence of the European peoples, we find that it lies in the great power given to us by the search for truth and its application to our daily lives.

I verily believe that in the advancement of science lies the hope of our civilization.

The benefits of science are not only material ones. The truths that science teaches are of common interest the world over. The language of science is universal, and is a powerful force in bringing the peoples of the world closer together. We are all acquainted with the sharp divisions which religions draw between men. In science there are no such divisions: all peoples worship at the shrine of truth. The spirit of science knows no national or religious boundaries, and it is thus a powerful force for the peace of the world.

The prize which you have given me today I consider the highest honor that a man can receive, for Nobel prizes have been a great stimulus to the advancement of science. In thanking you for the high honor you have conferred, I want also to congratulate the Swedish nation for having men of the far vision of Nobel, who could see clearly the importance to the world of encouraging the growth of science, and for having men with the enthusiasm and ability necessary to carry out Nobel's ideas and to extend them. Sweden has thus made good use of an unusual opportunity for stimulating science and for the promotion of international fellowship. Through her encouragement of science she has given us a greater hope for the future of our civilization.

I thank you.

# C.T.R. WILSON
# 1927

## INTRODUCTION

Charles Thomson Rees Wilson was born on the 14th of February, 1869, in the parish of Glencorse, near Edinburgh. His father, John Wilson, was a farmer, and his ancestors had been farmers in the South of Scotland for generations. His mother was Annie Clerk Harper.

At the age of four he lost his father, and his mother moved with the family to Manchester, where he was at first educated at a private school, and later at Owen's College - now the University of Manchester. Here, intending to become a physician, Wilson took up mainly biology. Having been granted an entrance scholarship in 1888 he went on to Cambridge (Sidney Sussex College), where he took his degree in 1892.

The immense increase of the "rain-like" condensation fitted excellently with the observation made by Thomson and McClelland immediately after Röntgen's discovery, that air was made conductive by the passage of X-rays.

Some of the most important achievements using the Wilson chamber were: the demonstration of the existence of Compton recoil electrons, thus establishing beyond any doubt the reality of the Compton effect (Compton shared the Nobel Prize with Wilson in 1927); the discovery of the positron by Anderson (who was awarded the Nobel Prize for 1936 for this feat); the visual demonstration of the processes of "pair creation" and "annihilation" of electrons and positrons by Blackett and Occhialini; and that of the transmutation of atomic nuclei carried out by Cockcroft and Walton.

In 1900, Wilson was made Fellow of Sidney Sussex College, and University Lecturer and Demonstrator. From then until 1918 he was in charge of the advanced teaching of practical physics at the Cavendish Laboratory, and also gave lectures on light.

In 1913, he was appointed Observer in Meteorological Physics at the Solar Physics Observatory, and most of his research both on the tracks of ionizing particles and on thunderstorm electricity was carried out there. In 1918, he was appointed Reader in Electrical Meteorology, and in 1925, Jacksonian Professor of Natural Philosophy. The Cambridge Philosophical Society awarded him the Hopkins Prize (1920), and the Royal Society of Edinburgh the Gunning Prize (1921), while the Franklin Institute presented him the Howard Potts Medal (1925).

After his retirement Wilson moved to Edinburgh, and later, at the age of 80, to the village of Carlops, close to his birthplace at the farmhouse of Crosshouse, at Glencorse.

He died on the 15th of November, 1959, in the midst of his family.

## PRIZE ACCEPTANCE SPEECH

*C. T. R. Wilson's speech at the Nobel Banquet in Stockholm, December 10, 1927*

*Your Royal Highnesses, Ladies and Gentlemen,*

I wish I could adequately express my gratitude to the Royal Swedish Academy of Science for the great honour they have conferred upon me.

I feel that I owe what success I have achieved in my scientific work mainly to my good fortune in beginning my experiments on clouds just at the right time - a few months before Röntgen made his great discovery.

And my choice of a subject to work upon was not due to any forethought on my own part nor to any good advice received, but just to the fact that in the autumn of 1894 I spent a few weeks on a cloudy Scottish hill-top - the top of Ben Nevis. Morning after morning I saw the sun rise above a sea of clouds and the shadow of the hill on the clouds below surrounded by gorgeous coloured rings. The beauty of what I saw made me fall in love with clouds and I made up my mind to make experiments to learn more about them.

Working in J. J. Thomson's laboratory during the years when X-rays and radio-activity were discovered, I could not help being interested in ions - and with ions and clouds I have worked ever since.

To those few weeks spent on the highest point of my native land I owe many happy years of work in the laboratory and not a few exciting moments - and perhaps my presence here tonight!

And perhaps I ought to tell how an experience on another Scottish hill was responsible for diverting my attention to another type of cloud than those condensed on ions in the laboratory - the thunder-cloud. While I stood on the top of a hill listening to the mutterings of distant thunder my hair suddenly rose up on end - and so my attention was very forcibly directed to the electric field of a thunder-cloud!

I am very glad to be associated with my friend Professor Compton in the award of the Nobel Prize for Physics. Compton was one of the workers in the Cavendish Laboratory a few years ago and in virtue of that we in Cambridge look upon him as one of ourselves.

Finally I should like to express my heartiest thanks to the Archbishop for all the kind things he has said, and to you all for your very kind welcome.

# OWEN WILLANS RICHARDSON
## 1928

### INTRODUCTION

Owen Willans Richardson was born on the 26th of April, 1879, at Dewsbury, Yorkshire, England, as the only son of Joshua Henry and Charlotte Maria Richardson. Educated at Batley Grammar School, he proceeded to Cambridge in 1897, having obtained an Entrance Major Scholarship at Trinity College; he gained First Class Honours in Natural Science at the examinations of the Universities of Cambridge and London, with particular distinctions in Physics and Chemistry. After graduating at Cambridge in 1900, he began to investigate the emission of electricity from hot bodies at the Cavendish Laboratory. In 1902 he was elected a Fellow of Trinity College, Cambridge. The law for the discovery of which the Nobel Prize was specially given, was first announced by him in a paper read before the Cambridge Philosophical Society on the 25th November, 1901, in the following words, as recorded in the published Proceedings: "If then the negative radiation is due to the corpuscles coming out of the metal, the saturation current s should obey the law $s = AT^{1/2}e^{-b/T}$. This law is fully confirmed by the experiments to be described." Richardson continued working at this subject at Cambridge until 1906, when he was appointed Professor of Physics at Princeton University in America, where he remained until the end of 1913, working at thermionic emission, photoelectric action, and the gyromagnetic effect. In 1911 he was elected a member of the American Philosophical Society, and in 1913 a Fellow of the Royal Society, whereupon (1914) he returned to England as Wheatstone Professor of Physics at King's College in the University of London. Among his publications were: *The Electron Theory of Matter*, 1914 (2nd ed., 1916), *The Emission of Electricity from Hot Bodies*, 1916 (2nd ed., 1921), *Molecular Hydrogen and its Spectrum*, 1934.

He was awarded the Hughes Medal by the Royal Society (1920), especially for work on thermionics; elected President, Section A, of the British Association (1921) and President of the Physical Society, London (1926-1928); appointed Yarrow Research Professor of the Royal Society, London (1926-1944), and knighted in 1939. Since 1914 he worked at thermionics, photoelectric effects, magnetism, the emission of electrons by chemical action, the theory of electrons, the quantum theory, the spectrum of molecular hydrogen, soft X-rays, the fine structure of Ha and Da. His last paper, with E. W. Foster, appeared in 1953. He received honorary degrees from the Universities of St. Andrews, Leeds, and London.

In 1906 he married Lilian Maud Wilson, the only sister of the well-known physicist H. A. Wilson, who was a fellow-student with him in Cambridge. There were two sons and one daughter of this marriage. After the death of his wife in 1945, Richardson married the physicist Henriette Rupp in 1948; he himself died in 1959.

## PRIZE ACCEPTANCE SPEECH

*Owen Willans Richardson's speech at the Nobel Banquet in Stockholm, December 10, 1929*

Your Royal Highnesses, Your Excellencies, My Lords, Ladies and Gentlemen,

I yield to no man in my admiration of the Swedish race. A race which has produced such names as those of Linnaeus, Scheele, Berzelius, Ångstrom and Rydberg, to mention a few only, is assured of the appreciation of every man of science. I willingly admit that Stockholm is one of the finest cities of the world. Indeed I am not prepared to quarrel with the assertion that it is the world's finest city. I also hope that, as one of the fortunate beneficiaries under his magnificent bequest, I am prepared to pay a fitting tribute to the genius and magnanimity of Alfred Nobel.

I will not, however, pursue these matters further. The same

theme has been admirably covered by my colleague Sir Frederick Hopkins. If I were to succeed in doing it better, I might be in danger of acquiring his perpetual enmity. If on the other hand I succeeded in doing it much worse, I might be equally in danger of losing, what I value much, your continued friendship.

No doubt you are aware, after the events of this afternoon, that I have the great honour of being the recipient of the Nobel Prize for Physics in 1928. But you are probably not aware, and I think this is an interesting fact, of the unusually close personal relationship between myself and the recipients of the Physics Prize for 1927. For one of them, Arthur Compton, was a research student of mine when I was at Princeton University, in America, and the other, C.T.R. Wilson, an old friend who was the best man at my wedding, an event which took place at an earlier stage of my career, in England. Now we in England are very interested in sporting events and in any unusual combination of circumstances. I feel that this particular combination of circumstances constitutes a record of successive personal association which is not likely to be broken for a very very long time.

Now Professor Harden has complained that until the award of the Nobel Prizes for 1929 Biochemistry has been regarded as the Cinderella of the Sciences. Well, I confess that I have sometimes secretly wished that Physics might suffer from a little, not too much, of the same malady. The trouble with Physics at the present time is that there are so many workers making discoveries so fast, and important discoveries too, that it is difficult for any one worker to keep a balanced view of the state of the subject. The fundamental principles also are in a very liquid state. For example, we often do not know whether to regard an electron as a particle, as in the older view, or as a wave, in accordance with the view of M. De Broglie, and if a wave, then a wave in what? Sometimes it seems to be a particle, sometimes a wave, and sometimes both. Certainly both these conceptions are necessary. Well, anyhow, I feel that order will ultimately come out of this chaos and very likely quite soon. As in other periods of intense scientific activity, we may confidently expect the ultimate results to be of great benefit to mankind.

In conclusion I wish to thank the Nobel Committee for their generous and indeed noble hospitality and all of you for the kind sympathy with which you have listened to my words.

# SIR VENKATA RAMAN
## 1930

### INTRODUCTION

Chandrasekhara Venkata Raman was born at Trichinopoly in Southern India on November 7th, 1888. His father was a lecturer in mathematics and physics so that from the first he was immersed in an academic atmosphere. He entered Presidency College, Madras, in 1902, and in 1904 passed his B.A. examination, winning the first place and the gold medal in physics; in 1907 he gained his M.A. degree, obtaining the highest distinctions.

His earliest researches in optics and acoustics - the two fields of investigation to which he has dedicated his entire career - were carried out while he was a student.

Since at that time a scientific career did not appear to present the best possibilities, Raman joined the Indian Finance Department in 1907; though the duties of his office took most of his time, Raman found opportunities for carrying on experimental research in the laboratory of the Indian Association for the Cultivation of Science at Calcutta (of which he became Honorary Secretary in 1919).

In 1917 he was offered the newly endowed Palit Chair of Physics at Calcutta University, and decided to accept it. After 15 years at Calcutta he became Professor at the Indian Institute of Science at Bangalore (1933-1948), and since 1948 he is Director of the Raman Institute of Research at Bangalore, established and endowed by himself. He also founded the *Indian Journal of Physics* in 1926, of which he is the Editor. Raman sponsored the establishment of the Indian Academy of Sciences and has served as President since its inception. He also initiated the *Proceedings* of that academy, in which much of his work has been published, and is President of the Current Science Association, Bangalore, which publishes *Current Science (India)*.

Some of Raman's early memoirs appeared as Bulletins of the *Indian Associationfor the Cultivation of Science* (Bull. 6 and 11, dealing with the "Maintenance of Vibrations"; Bull. 15, 1918, dealing with the theory of the musical instruments of the violin family). He contributed an article on the theory of musical instruments to the 8th Volume of the *Handbuch der Physik*, 1928. In 1922 he published his work on the "Molecular Diffraction of Light", the first of a series of investigations with his collaborators which ultimately led to his discovery, on the 28th of February, 1928, of the radiation effect which bears his name ("A new radiation", *Indian J. Phys.*, 2 (1928) 387), and which gained him the 1930 Nobel Prize in Physics.

Other investigations carried out by Raman were: his experimental and theoretical studies on the diffraction of light by acoustic waves of ultrasonic and hypersonic frequencies (published 1934-1942), and those on the effects produced by X-rays on infrared vibrations in crystals exposed to ordinary light. In 1948 Raman, through studying the spectroscopic behaviour of crystals, approached in a new manner fundamental problems of crystal dynamics. His laboratory has been dealing with the structure and properties of diamond, the structure and optical behaviour of numerous iridescent substances (labradorite, pearly felspar, agate, opal, and pearls).

Among his other interests have been the optics of colloids, electrical and magnetic anisotropy, and the physiology of human vision.

Raman has been honoured with a large number of honorary doctorates and memberships of scientific societies. He was elected a Fellow of the Royal Society early in his career (1924), and was knighted in 1929.

## PRIZE ACCEPTANCE SPEECH

## December 11, 1930

**The Molecular Scattering of Light**

The colour of the sea

In the history of science, we often find that the study of some natural phenomenon has been the starting-point in the development of a new branch of knowledge. We have an instance of this in the colour of skylight, which has inspired numerous optical investigations, and the explanation of which, proposed by the late Lord Rayleigh, and subsequently verified by observation, forms the beginning of our knowledge of the subject of this lecture. Even more striking, though not so familiar to all, is the colour exhibited by oceanic waters. A voyage to Europe in the summer of 1921 gave me the first opportunity of observing the wonderful blue opalescence of the Mediterranean Sea. It seemed not unlikely that the phenomenon owed its origin to the scattering of sunlight by the molecules of the water. To test this explanation, it appeared desirable to ascertain the laws governing the diffusion of light in liquids, and experiments with this object were started immediately on my return to Calcutta in September, 1921. It soon became evident, however, that the subject possessed a significance extending far beyond the special purpose for which the work was undertaken, and that it offered unlimited scope for research. It seemed indeed that the study of light-scattering might carry one into the deepest problems of physics and chemistry, and it was this belief which led to the subject becoming the main theme of our activities at Calcutta from that time onwards.

*The theory of fluctuations*

From the work of the first few months, it became clear that the molecular scattering of light was a very general phenomenon which could be studied not only in gases and vapours but also in liquids and in crystalline and amorphous solids, and that it was primarily an effect arising from molecular disarray in the medium and consequent local fluctuations in its optical density. Except in amorphous solids, such molecular disarray could presumably be ascribed to thermal agitation, and the experimental results appeared to support this view. The fact that molecules are optically anisotropic and can orientate freely in liquids was found to give rise to an additional type of scattering. This could be distinguished from the scattering due to fluctuations in density by reason of its being practically unpolarized, whereas the latter was completely polarized in the transverse direction. The whole subject was critically reviewed and the results till then obtained were set out in an essay published by the Calcutta University Press in February 1922. The various problems requiring solution indicated in this essay were investigated with the aid of a succession of able collaborators. It is possible to mention briefly only a few of the numerous investigations which were carried out at Calcutta during the six years 1922 to 1927. The scattering of light in fluids was studied by Ramanathan over a wide range of pressures and temperatures with results which appeared to support the "fluctuation" theory of its origin. His work also disclosed the remarkable changes in the state of polarization which accompany the variations of intensity with temperature in vapours and in liquids. Liquid mixtures were investigated by Kameswara Rao, and furnished optical proof of the existence in such systems, of simultaneous fluctuations of density, composition, and molecular orientation. Srivastava studied the scattering of light in crystals in relation to the thermal fluctuations of density and their increase with temperature. Ramdas investigated the scattering of light by liquid surfaces due to thermal agitation, and established a relation between surface-tension and surface-opalescence. He also traced the transition from surface-opalescence to volume-opalescence which occurs at the critical temperature. Sogani investigated X-ray diffraction in liquids, in order to connect it with their optical behaviour, and test the application of fluctuation theory to X-ray scattering.

*The anisotropy of molecules*

As stated above, the state of polarization of the light scattered in fluids is connected with the optical anisotropy of the molecules. Much of the work done at Calcutta during the years 1922 to 1927 was intended to obtain data concerning this property and to establish its relations with various optical phenomena. Krishnan examined a great many liquids, and by his work showed very clearly the dependence of the optical anisotropy of the molecule on its chemical constitution. Ramakrishna Rao studied the depolarization of scattered light in a very large number of gases and vapours, and obtained information of high importance for the progress of the subject. Venkateswaran studied the scattering of light in aqueous solutions to find the influence on it of electrolytic dissociation. Ramachandra Rao investigated liquids having highly elongated molecules and also highly polar substances over a wide range of temperatures, and discovered the influence of molecular shape and molecular association on the depolarization of scattered light in liquids.

The interpretation of the observations with liquids involved the development of a molecular theory of light-scattering in dense media which was undertaken by Ramanathan, myself, and Krishnan. A revised opalescence formula was derived which differed from that of Einstein and yielded results in better agreement with observation. Krishnan and myself also published a series of investigations showing how the optical anisotropy of the molecules deduced from light-scattering could be utilized to interpret the optical and dielectric behaviour of fluids, and also the electric, magnetic, and mechanical birefringence exhibited by them.

The conclusions derived from these studies enabled a connection to be established between the molecular anisotropy observed in fluids and the optical, electric, and magnetic aeolotropy exhibited by solids in the crystalline state.

The investigations referred to above were in the main guided by the classical electromagnetic theory of light, the application of which to the problems of light-scattering is chiefly associated with the names of Rayleigh and of Einstein.

Nevertheless, the possibility that the corpuscular nature of light might come into evidence in scattering was not overlooked and was in fact elaborately discussed in the essay of February 1922 which was published at least a year before the well-known discoveries of Compton on X-ray scattering.

While our experiments in the main appeared to support the electromagnetic theory of light, evidence came to hand at a very early stage of the investigations of the existence of a phenomenon which seemed to stand outside the classical scheme of thought. The scattering of light in transparent fluids is extremely feeble, much weaker in fact than the Tyndall effect usually observed in turbid media. It was experimentally discovered that associated with the Rayleigh-Einstein type of molecular scattering, was another and still feebler type of secondary radiation, the intensity of which was of the order of magnitude of a few hundredths of the classical scattering, and differed from it in not having the same wavelength as the primary or incident radiation.

The first observation of this phenomenon was made at Calcutta in April 1923 by Ramanathan who was led to it in attempting to explain why in certain liquids (water, ether, methyl and ethyl alcohols), the depolarization of scattered light varied with the wavelength of the incident radiation.

Ramanathan found that after exhaustive chemical purification and repeated slow distillation of the liquid in vacuum, the new radiation persisted undiminished in intensity, showing that it was a characteristic property of the substance studied and not due to any fluorescent impurity. Krishnan observed a similar effect in many other liquids in 1924, and a somewhat more conspicuous phenomenon was observed by me in ice and in optical glasses.

The optical analogue of the Compton effect

The origin of this puzzling phenomenon naturally interested us, and in the summer of 1925, Venkateswaran attempted to investigate it by photographing the spectrum of the scattered light from liquids, using sunlight filtered through colour screens, but was unable to report any decisive results. Ramakrishna

Rao in his studies on the depolarization of scattering during 1926 and 1927 looked carefully for a similar phenomenon in gases and vapours, but without success. This problem was taken up again by Krishnan towards the end of 1927. While his work was in progress, the first indication of the true nature of the phenomenon came to hand from a different quarter. One of the problems interesting us at this time was the behaviour in light-scattering of highly viscous organic liquids which were capable of passing over into the glassy state. Venkateswaran undertook to study this question, and reported the highly interesting result that the colour of sunlight scattered in a highly purified sample of glycerine was a brilliant green instead of the usual blue. The phenomenon appeared to be similar to that discovered by Ramanathan in water and the alcohols, but of much greater intensity, and, therefore, more easily studied. No time was lost in following up the matter. Tests were made with a series of filters transmitting narrow regions of the solar spectrum and placed in the path of the incident beam, which showed that in every case the colour of the scattered light was different from that of the incident light, and was displaced from it towards the red. The radiations were also strongly polarized. These facts indicated a clear analogy between the empirical characters of the phenomenon and the Compton effect. The work of Compton had made familiar the idea that the wavelength of radiation could be degraded in the process of scattering, and the observations with glycerine suggested to me that the phenomenon which had puzzled us ever since 1923 was in fact the optical analogue of the Compton effect. This idea naturally stimulated further investigation with other substances.

The chief difficulty which had hitherto oppressed us in the study of the new phenomenon was its extreme feebleness in general. This was overcome by using a 7-inch refracting telescope in combination with a short-focus lens to condense sunlight into a pencil of very great intensity. With these arrangements and using complementary light-filters in the path of the incident and scattered beams, as was done by Ramanathan in 1923, to isolate the modified radiations, it was found that they could be readily observed in a great many liquids, and that in many cases they were strongly polarized.

Krishnan, who very materially assisted me in these investigations, found at the same time that the phenomenon could be observed in several organic vapours, and even succeeded in visually determining the state of polarization of the modified radiations from them. Compressed gases such as CO, and N2O, crystalline ice, and optical glasses also were found to exhibit the modified radiations. These observations left little doubt that the phenomenon was really a species of light-scattering analogous to the Compton effect.

*The spectroscopic characters of the new effect*

Thanks to the vastly more powerful illumination made available by the 7- inch refractor, the spectroscopic examination of the effect, which had been abandoned in 1925 as indecisive, now came within the reach of direct visual study. With a Zeiss cobalt-glass filter placed in the path of the incident beam and one or other of a series of organic liquids as the scattering substance, a band in the blue-green region was observed by me in the spectrum of the scattered light, separated by a dark interval from the indigo-violet region transmitted by the filter. *Both* of these regions in the spectrum became sharper when the region of transmission was narrowed by the insertion of an additional filter in the incident beam. This suggested the employment, instead of sunlight, of the highly monochromatic radiations given by a mercury arc in combination with a condenser of large aperture and a cobalt-glass filter.

With these arrangements the spectrum of the scattered light from a variety of liquids and solids was visually examined, and the startling observation was made that the spectrum generally included a number of sharp lines or bands on a diffuse background which were not present in the light of the mercury arc.

The quartz mercury lamp was so powerful and convenient a source of monochromatic illumination that, at least in the case of liquids and solids, photographing the spectrum of scattered light was found to present no extraordinary difficulties. The earliest pictures of the phenomenon were in fact taken with a portable quartz spectrograph of the smallest size made by the firm of Hilger. With a somewhat larger instrument of the same type, Krishnan obtained very satisfactory spectrograms with liquids and with crystals on which measurements of the desired precision could be made, and on which the presence of lines displaced towards the violet was first definitely established. The experimental difficulties were naturally greater in the case of gases or vapours, though they could be lessened by working with the substance under pressure. With an improvised instrument of large aperture Ramdas obtained the first spectrograms with a gaseous substance (ether vapour) at atmospheric pressure.

In interpreting the observed phenomena, the analogy with the Compton effect was adopted as the guiding principle. The work of Compton had gained general acceptance for the idea that the scattering of radiation is a unitary process in which the conservation principles hold good. Accepting this idea it follows at once that, if the scattering particle gains any energy during the encounter with the quantum, the latter is deprived of energy to the same extent, and accordingly appears after scattering as a radiation of diminished frequency. From thermodynamic principles, it follows that the reverse process should also be possible. Adopting these ideas, the actual observations could be interpreted, and the agreement of the observed displacements with the infrared frequencies of the molecules made it clear that the new method opened up an illimitable field of experimental research in the study of the structure of matter.

*Interpretation of the effect*

It appears desirable to emphasize that though the

conservation principle of Compton is useful in interpreting the effects disclosed by experiment, it is by itself insufficient to explain the observed phenomena. As is well known from studies on molecular spectra, a gaseous molecule has four different species of energy of increasing orders of magnitude, namely those corresponding to translatory motion, rotation, vibration, and electronic excitation. Each of these, except the first, is quantized and may be represented by an integer in an extended sequence of quantum numbers. The aggregate energy of a molecule may, therefore, assume any one out of a very large number of possible values. If we assume that an exchange of energy occurs in the collision between the molecule and the quantum, and limit ourself to the cases in which the final energy of the molecule is less than that of the incident quantum, we arrive at the result that the spectrum of the scattered light should contain an immense number of new lines and should in fact rival in its complexity the band spectrum of the molecule observed in the emission or absorption of light.

Nothing more different from what is actually observed can be imagined than the foregoing picture. The most conspicuous feature revealed by experiment is the beautiful simplicity of the spectra of even complicated polyatomic molecules obtained in light-scattering, a simplicity that is in striking contrast to the extreme complexity of their emission or absorption spectra. It is this simplicity that gives to the study of light-scattering its special significance and value. It is clear that the effect actually observed was not and could not have been foreseen from an application of the conservation principles.

The general principle of correspondence between the quantum and classical theories enunciated by Niels Bohr enables us, on the other hand, to obtain a real insight into the actual phenomena. The classical theory of lightscattering tells us that if a molecule scatters light while it is moving, rotating or vibrating, the scattered radiations may include certain frequencies, different from those of the incident waves. This classical picture, in many respects, is surprisingly like what we actually observe in the experiments. It explains why the frequency shifts observed fall into three classes, translational, rotational and vibrational, of different orders of magnitude.

It explains the observed selection rules, as for instance, why the frequencies of vibration deduced from scattered light include only the fundamentals and not the overtones and combinations which are so conspicuous in emission and absorption spectra. The classical theory can even go further and give us a rough indication of the intensity and polarization of the radiations of altered frequency.

Nevertheless, the classical picture has to be modified in essential respects to give even a qualitative description of the phenomena, and we have, therefore, to invoke the aid of quantum principles.

The work of Kramers and Heisenberg, and the newer developments in quantum mechanics which have their root in Bohr's correspondence principle seem to offer a promising way of approach towards an understanding of the experimental results. But until we know much more than we do at present regarding the structure of molecules, and have sufficient quantitative experimental knowledge of the effect, it would be rash to suggest that they afford a complete explanation of it.

The significance of the effect

The universality of the phenomenon, the convenience of the experimental technique and the simplicity of the spectra obtained enable the effect to be used as an experimental aid to the solution of a wide range of problems in physics and chemistry.

Indeed, it may be said that it is this fact which constitutes the principal significance of the effect. The frequency differences determined from the spectra, the width and character of the lines appearing in them, and the intensity and state of polarization of the scattered radiations enable us to obtain an insight into the ultimate structure of the scattering substance. As experimental research has shown, these features in the spectraare very definitely influenced by physical conditions, such as temperature and state of aggregation, by physico-chemical conditions, such as mixture, solution, molecular association and polymerization, and most essentially by chemical constitution.

It follows that the new field of spectroscopy has practically unrestricted scope in the study of problems relating to the structure of matter. We may also hope that it will lead us to a fuller understanding of the nature of light, and of the interactions between matter and light.

*Some concluding remarks*

From a physical point of view, the quantitative study of the effect with the simplest molecules holds out the largest hope of fundamental advances. The beautiful work of McLennan with liquefied gases, and of R. W. Wood and Rasetti are pioneer investigations in this field which command the highest admiration. The quantitative study of the effect with crystals of the simplest possible chemical constitution is naturally of great importance. The case of the diamond, which has been investigated by Ramaswamy, Robertson, and

Fox, and with especial completeness by Bhagavantam, is of special interest. Very surprising results have been obtained with this substance, which may be the pathway to a fuller understanding of the nature of the crystalline state.

I should also like to draw attention to the work of Krishnamurti, who has traced a remarkable dependence of the intensity of the spectral lines observed in scattering on the nature of the chemical bond, and followed the transition from the homopolar to the heteropolar type of chemical combination. Krishnamurti's observation that the paramagnetism of crystals apparently influences the observed intensity of the displaced lines is one of the most remarkable ever made in this new field of research.

# CLINTON DAVISSON
## 1937

### INTRODUCTION

Clinton Joseph Davisson was born at Bloomington, Illinois, U.S.A., October 22, 1881, son of Joseph Davisson, an artisan, native of Ohio, descendant of early Dutch and French settlers of Virginia, Union veteran of the American Civil War, and Mary Calvert, a school-teacher, native of Pennsylvania, of English and Scotch parentage.

He attended the Bloomington public schools, and on graduation from High School in 1902 was granted a scholarschip by the University of Chicago for proficiency in mathematics and physics. In January 1904 he was appointed assistant in physics at Purdue University on recommendation of Professor Millikan. He returned to Chicago in June 1904 and remained in residence at the University until August 1905. In September 1905, again on the recommendation of Professor Millikan, he was appointed part-time instructor in physics at Princeton University. This post he held until 1910, studying, as his duties permitted, under Professor Francis Magie, Professor E. P. Adams, Professor ( later Sir ) James Jeans and particularly under Professor O.W. Richardson. During a part of this period Davisson returned to the University of Chicago for the summer sessions and in August 1908 received a B.S. degree from that institution.

He was awarded a Fellowship in Physics at Princeton for the year 1910-1911 and during that year completed requirements for the degree of Ph.D. which he received dune 1911. From September 1911 until June 1917 he was an instructor in the Department of Physics at the Carnegie Institute of Technology, Pittsburgh, Pa. During the summer of 1913 he worked in the Cavendish Laboratory under Professor (later Sir) J.J. Thomson.

From 1930-1937 Dr. Davisson devoted himself to the study of the theory of electron optics and to applications of this theory to engineering problems. He then investigated the scattering and reflection of very slow electrons by metals. During World War II he worked on the theory of electronic devices and on a variety of crystal physics problems.

In 1928 he was awarded the Comstock Prize by the National Academy of Sciences, in 1931 the Elliott Cresson Medal by the Franklin Institute, and in 1935 the Hughes Medal by the Royal Society (London), and in 1941 the Alumni Medal by the University of Chicago. He held honorary doctorates from Purdue University, Princeton University, the University of Lyon and Colby College.

In 1911 he married Charlotte Sara Richardson, a sister of Professor Richardson. He died in Charlottesville on February 1, 1958, at the age of 76, and was survived by his wife, three sons and one daughter.

## PRIZE ACCEPTANCE SPEECH

*Clinton Davisson's speech at the Nobel Banquet in Stockholm, December 10, 1937*

*Royal Highnesses, Ladies and Gentlemen:*

Before coming to Stockholm I talked in London with Professor and Mrs. Thomson who regret exceedingly their inability to be here on this great occasion. It is Professor Thomson's desire that the spirit of my remarks be taken as expressing his sentiments as well as my own.

I welcome this opportunity of assuring you that I appreciate most deeply, prize most highly the great honor which His Majesty, Your King, conferred upon me in the impressive ceremonies of a few hours since.

Great as is my pleasure in accepting, jointly with my friend, Professor Thomson, this year's Nobel Prize for Physics, the pleasure is made greater still by the joy it brings to countless numbers of my fellow countrymen, to my family, to my colleagues and hundreds of associates in the great industrial laboratories in which I work, to the physicists of America and to thousands of patriotic Americans who regard it as a most notable recognition of their country.

I have wondered at times during the last month, if the people of Sweden fully realize the great importance attached to Nobel prize awards by the people of the United States. I hardly realized it myself a month ago. The recipient is transformed overnight from, in my case, an exceedingly private citizen to something in the nature of a semi-public institution.

This, I think, is not exactly the result which Alfred Nobel sought to achieve by his last will and testament. His aim, it seems, was merely and quite simply to provide substantial reward for high achievement in certain laudable fields of endeavor - achievements which are made, not primarily for gain, which are beneficial to mankind, but which mankind does not, in the usual course of events, pay for.

In particular Nobel seems to have had no thought of dispensing special honor or distinction to the winners of his prizes. These intangibles which have so increased in value with the years must be regarded, I think, as precious byproducts which Nobel did not envisage. That they should come to rate so highly in the world, as today they do, was, indeed, by no means inevitable. Their great value derives quite definitely from the thorough, ceaseless labors of long lines of Nobel Prize Committees - Committees which for years have commanded the respect, the confidence and the admiration of the educated classes of all countries.

It is exceedingly fortunate that Nobel was a Swede. For what people other than the Swedish were so endowed by their freedom from international entanglements, by the liberality of their views, and by the breadth of their tolerance to organize and administer the precious trust which Alfred Nobel gave into their hands?

In conclusion, allow me to thank most sincerely everyone concerned, and this, I take it, means everyone in Sweden, for the tangible as well as the intangible rewards which you have bestowed upon me. Let me thank you, also most sincerely, for the warmth of the welcome you have extended to Mrs Davisson and me on this our first, but I trust not our last, visit to your wonderful and beautiful Sweden.

# ERNEST LAWRENCE
## 1939

### INTRODUCTION

Ernest Orlando Lawrence was born on 8th August, 1901, at Canton, South Dakota (United States). His early education was at Canton High School, then St. Olaf College. In 1919 he went to the University of South Dakota, receiving his B.A. in Chemistry in 1922. The following year he received his M.A. from the University of Minnesota. He spent a year at Chicago University doing physics and was awarded his Ph.D. from Yale University in 1925. He continued at Yale for a further three years, the first two as a National Research Fellow and the third as Assistant Professor of Physics. In 1928 he was appointed Associate Professor of Physics at the University of California, Berkeley, and two years later he became Professor, being the youngest professor at Berkeley. In 1936 he became Director of the University's Radiation Laboratory as well, remaining in these posts until his death.

During World War II he made vital contributions to the development of the atomic bomb, holding several official appointments in the project. After the war he played a part in the attempt to obtain international agreement on the suspension of atomic-bomb testing, being a member of the U.S. delegation at the 1958 Geneva Conference on this subject.

Lawrence's research centred on nuclear physics. His early work was on ionization phenomena and the measurement of ionization potentials of metal vapours. In 1929 he invented the cyclotron, a device for accelerating nuclear particles to very high velocities without the use of high voltages. The swiftly moving particles were used to bombard atoms of various elements, disintegrating the atoms to form, in some cases, completely new elements. Hundreds of radioactive isotopes of the known elements were also discovered. His brother, Dr. John Lawrence, who became Director of the University's Medical Physics Laboratory, collaborated with him in studying medical and biological applications of the cyclotron and himself became a consultant to the Institute of Cancer Research at Columbia.

Larger and more powerful versions of the cyclotron were built by Lawrence. In 1941 the instrument was used to generate artificially the cosmic particles called mesons, and later the studies were extended to antiparticles.

Lawrence was a most prolific writer: during 1924-1940 his name appeared on 56 papers (an average of $3^1/_2$ papers a year), showing his exceptional breadth of interest. He was also the inventor of a method for obtaining time intervals as small as three billionths of a second, to study the discharge phenomena of an electric spark. In addition he devised a very precise method for measuring the $e/m$ ratio of the electron, one of the fundamental constants of Nature. Most of his work was published in *The Physical Review* and the *Proceedings of the National Academy of Sciences.*

Among his many awards may be mentioned the Elliott Cresson Medal of the Franklin Institute, the Comstock Prize of the National Academy of Sciences, the Hughes Medal of the Royal Society, the Duddell Medal of the Royal Physical Society, the Faraday Medal, and the Enrico Fermi Award. He was decorated with the Medal for Merit and was an Officer of the Legion of Honour. He held honorary doctorates of thirteen American and one British University (Glasgow). He was a member or fellow of many American and foreign learned societies.

Lawrence married Mary Kimberly Blumer, daughter of the Emeritus Dean at Yale Medical School, in May 1932. They had six children. His recreations were boating, tennis, ice-skating, and music. He died on 27th August, 1958, at Palo Alto, California.

## PRIZE ACCEPTANCE SPEECH

*Ernest Lawrence's speech from the ceremony in Berkeley, February 29, 1940*

*Mr. President, Mr. Consul-General, Professor Birge, Ladies and Gentlemen!*

Words fail me in giving expression to my thoughts on this occasion. To convey to you, Mr. Consul-General, and through you to the Royal Swedish Academy of Science my profound gratitude for this great honor would be giving expression to only a part of what is in my mind; for I am mindful that scientific achievement is rooted in the past, is cultivated to full stature by many contemporaries and flourishes only in favorable environment. No individual is alone responsible for a single stepping stone along the path of progress, and where the path is smooth progress is most rapid. In my own work this has been particularly true. From the beginning of the Radiation Laboratory, I have had the rare good fortune of being in the center of a group of men of high ability, enthusiastic and completely devoted to scientific pursuits. I wish it were possible this evening for me to pay tribute individually to them all, for it was our joint endeavors which have made possible the work which has been so magnificently recognized by the Nobel Award; but I must content myself with accepting this great honor with the happy thought that I am the representative of these valued associates and friends.

I know also that I speak for my colleagues in the Radiation Laboratory as well as for myself when I take this felicitous opportunity to acknowledge with sincere gratitude the generous help we have received from many sources. The day when the scientist, no matter how devoted, may make significant progress alone and without material help is past. This fact is most self-evident in our work. Instead of an attic with a few test tubes, bits of wire and odds and ends, the attack on the atomic nucleus has required the development and construction of great instruments on an engineering scale. This has been possible only through generous assistance from several quarters - notably the Research Corporation, the Chemical Foundation, the Rockefeller Foundation, and from the late William H. Crocker, Regent of the University. These benefactors share the honor of this occasion because without their help the work of our laboratory could not have been brought to its present fruition.

I have suggested that scientific progress requires a favorable environment. The University of California rightfully takes pride in the Nobel Award because the University as a whole has contributed immeasurably in diverse ways to the work of the Radiation Laboratory. I shall always be grateful for the wise and generous guidance and help that our work has received from the University Board of Research, and especially from Professor Leuschner, Chairman of the Research Board, in the early years of organization of the laboratory, and above all may I acknowledge my deep appreciation of the support of the President of the University, who whole-heartedly has been all along such a stimulus to our activities. It may truly be said that this Nobel Award is yet another tribute to his great academic leadership.

It is a source of gratification to us all that we have been able to contribute a little to an understanding of the nucleus of the atom. We are glad that already in these early beginnings discoveries have emerged of immediate practical significance - for, as Professor Birge has so graciously said this evening, the new radiations and radioactive substances have opened vistas for all the sciences, especially in medical research and therapy. In the Radiation Laboratory we count it a privilege to do everything we can to assist our medical colleagues in the application of these new tools to the problems of human suffering.

At the same time we have been looking towards the new frontier in the atom, the domain of energies above a hundred million volts, for we have every reason to believe that there lies ahead for exploration a territory with treasures transcending anything thus far unearthed. To penetrate this new frontier will require the building of a giant cyclotron, perhaps weighing more than 4,000 tons - twenty times larger than the new medical cyclotron of the Crocker Laboratory. We have been working on the designs of such a great instrument and are convinced that there are no insurmountable technical difficulties in the way of producing atomic projectiles of energies well above one hundred million volts, but of course such a great instrument would involve large expenditures. Perhaps I might say that the difficulties in the way of crossing the next frontier in the atom are no longer in our laboratory. They constitute a very considerable financial problem, which we must hand over to President Sproul.

Professor Birge has alluded to the very great importance of this project. As he has indicated, there are substantial prospects that it will be the instrumentality for finding the key to the almost limitless reservoir of energy in the heart of the atom. Certainly, it may bring to light such a deeper knowledge of the structure of matter as to constitute a veritable discontinuity in the progress of science.

Therefore, Mr. Consul-General, I believe that in this instance the award of the Nobel Prize is accomplishing to an unusual degree the purpose intended by Alfred Nobel - the encouragement of fundamental scientific research. For it goes without saying that this great recognition at this time will aid tremendously our efforts to find the necessarily large funds for the next voyage of exploration farther into the depths of the atom. Let us cherish the hope that the day is not far distant when we will be in the midst of this next adventure.

In closing, may I again give expression to a profound feeling of gratitude and appreciation for this great honor, which I share with the University and with all those outside who have contributed to make our work possible and above all with my valued colleagues and co-workers, both past and present.

# PERCY W. BRIDGMAN
## 1946

### INTRODUCTION

Percy Williams Bridgman was born in Cambridge, Massachusetts, on April 21st, 1882. He received his early education in public schools in the nearby city of Newton until 1900 when he entered Harvard University. He graduated A.B. in 1904, A.M. in 1905 and was awarded his Ph.D. (Physics) in 1908 when he joined the Faculty of the University. Bridgman was successively appointed Instructor (1910), Assistant Professor (1919), before becoming Hollis Professor of Mathematics and Natural Philosophy in 1926. He was appointed Higgins University Professor in 1950.

His researches concerning the effects of high pressures on materials and their thermodynamic behaviour commenced in 1905 and have continued throughout his career. He has carried out extensive investigations on the properties of matter at pressures up to 100,000 atmosphere including a study of the compressibility, electric and thermal conductivity, tensile strength and viscosity of more than 100 different compounds. He developed a method of packing which eliminated leak, and later introduced various methods of external support to pressure vessels as higher pressures were demanded. Bridgman has also contributed to crystallography, where he devised a method of growing single crystals; to the problems of electrical conduction in metals, where he discovered internal

Peltier heat - a new electrical effect; and to the philosophy of modern physics. In the latter field, he is a strong supporter of the operational viewpoint, considering it meaningless to interpret physical concepts except as they are capable of observation.

Prof. Bridgman has contributed many papers to leading scientific journals and he is the author of *Dimensional Analysis* (1922), *The Logic of Modern Physics* (1927), *The Physics of High Pressure* (1931), *The Thermodynamics of Electrical Phenomena in Metals* (1934), *The Nature of Physical Theory* (1936), *The Intelligent Individual and Society* (1938), *The Nature of Thermodynamics* (1941), and, more recently, *Refections of a Physicist.*

He has received honorary Doctor of Science degrees from Stevens Institute (1934), Harvard (1939), Brooklyn Polytechnic (1941), Princeton (1950), Paris (1950), and Yale (1951). He has received the Rumford Medal (American Academy of Arts and Sciences), the Cresson Medal (Franklin Institute), the Roozeboom Medal (Royal Academy of Sciences of the Netherlands), the Comstock Prize (National Academy of Sciences), and the New York Award of the Research Corporation. He was a member of the American Physical Society (President, 1942), the American Association for the Advancement of Science, the American Academy of Arts and Sciences, the American Philosophical Society, and the National Academy of Sciences. He was a Foreign Member of the Royal Society and Honorary Fellow of the Physical Society (London).

Bridgman married Olive Ware in 1912. Their daughter, Jane, was born in I9I4, and their son, Robert Ware, in 1915.

Prof. Bridgman died in 1961.

## PRIZE ACCEPTANCE SPEECH

*Percy W. Bridgman's speech at the Nobel Banquet in Stockholm, December 10, 1946*

It is my pleasant duty on behalf of my colleagues in physics, Messrs. Pauli and Stern, as well as on my own behalf, to express our deep appreciation and gratitude for the high honor that has been bestowed upon us. It is, I think, the universal opinion among physicists that a physicist may attain no higher single honor than the Nobel award.

We are also keenly conscious of the arduous labor which the bestowing of these awards imposes on the Nobel Committee. We are grateful to them, and hope that they may feel that their labors have to some extent been justified.

In the United States one often hears the remark that of all the countries of the world Sweden is the most civilized. Not the least of the evidence of this civilization is the provision for the Nobel awards. Alfred Nobel surely displayed the highest wisdom in establishing these prizes. It would not be possible to overestimate the effect which they have had in stimulating the growth of science in all countries, and in promoting the feeling of universal brotherhood among scientists. Not only has science itself been stimulated, but also the cause of peace. There would be no more worthy recipient of his own peace prize than Alfred Nobel because of the indirect effect of his encouragement of science.

Finally it remains to express our deep appreciation of the courtesy and hospitality of all whom we have met in Stockholm. In this you have achieved the supreme success of making us feel that you have *enjoyed* extending your hospitality. We shall never forget the pleasure you have given us.

# EDWARD V. APPLETON
# 1947

## INTRODUCTION

Edward Victor Appleton was born in Bradford, England, on 6th Sep., 1892, the son of Peter and Mary Appleton. He received his early education at Hanson Grammar School. Bradford then took his B.A. degree in Natural Science at St. John's College, Cambridge, in 1913 and 1914, with physics for Part II. He won the Wiltshire Prize in 1913 and the Hutchinson Research Studentship in 1914, studying under Sir J.J. Thomson and Lord Rutherford. During the First World War he joined the West Riding Regiment, transferring later to the Royal Engineers. At the conclusion of hostilities he returned to Cambridge and took up research on radio waves.

Since 1919 Appleton has devoted himself to scientific problems in atmospheric physics, using mainly radio techniques. In 1920 he was appointed assistant demonstrator in experimental physics at the Cavendish Laboratory. Two years later he became sub-rector at Trinity College.

In 1924 Appleton was appointed Professor of Physics at London University and served there for twelve years, returning to Cambridge in 1936 to take the Chair of Natural Philosophy.

Further experiments which led to the possibility of round-the-world broadcasting were carried out and in 1926 he discovered a further atmospheric layer 150 miles above ground, higher than the Heaviside Layer and electrically stronger. In 1932 he was elected Vice-President of the American Institute of Radio

Engineers.

When hostilities broke out in 1939 Appleton was appointed Secretary of the Department of Scientific and Industrial Research - the senior British Government post concerned with physical science.

In 1947, the year in which he received the Nobel Prize for Physics, he was also awarded the highest civilian decoration of the United States - the Medal of Merit - and was made an Officer of the French Legion of Honour. He was also awarded the Norwegian Cross of Freedom for his war work. Appleton's work has been recognized by India, Norway and Denmark, and in 1948 he was appointed by the Pope to the Pontificial Academy of Science. He received the Albert Medal of the Royal Society of Arts, in 1950, for outstanding services to science and industrial research and was elected President of the British Association for the Advancement of Science for the Liverpool meeting in 1953.

In 1956 Sir Edward gave the Reith Lectures of the B.B.C. on "Science and the Nation". Recent awards made to him have been the Gunning Victoria Jubilee Prize of the Royal Society, Edinburgh, in 1960, and the Medal of Honour of the Institute of Radio Engineers of America in 1962.

In 1915 Appleton married Jessie, daughter of the Rev. J. Longson, and they have two daughters.

## PRIZE ACCEPTANCE SPEECH

*Edward V. Appleton's speech at the Nobel Banquet in Stockholm, December 10, 1947*

*Your Royal Highness, Your Excellencies, Ladies and Gentlemen:*

I wish to thank you, Professor Tiselius, for the kind and generous way in which you have commended us to the distinguished gathering assembled here tonight; and I want to thank all of you for the warm response you have given to the toast. Your kindness has made me discover a new characteristic of human beings, and that is that it is possible for a person to feel both humble and proud at the same time! I feel humble because I know how much my scientific work has been dependent on the cooperation and assistance of so many people and organisations, of which I am, tonight, the fortunate representative. But I am certainly proud to stand here with my good friend Sir Robert Robinson, the President of our own Royal Society in Britain, and with my distinguished colleagues from the United States and Argentina.

Perhaps you will understand me when I say that I much regret that my old professor, Lord Rutherford, a Nobel Prizeman himself, who gave me the warmest encouragement and help when I began to work on the ionosphere, is not alive today to let me hear his own words of approval.

For the period of the war, in my own country, it was necessary, and regrettably so, for scientific workers to devote their whole time to the applications of existing scientific knowledge. But, with the return of peace, there has been a great change, and fundamental research, designed to extend the endless frontier of knowledge, is now again receiving the attention it deserves. The English philosopher, Francis Bacon, distinguished between what he called *experimenta fructifera* - fruitful experiments - and *experimenta lucifera* -light-giving experiments. In the extension of science for the welfare of mankind we clearly want both kinds of experiments, for the light-giving experiments of which Bacon spoke, although prompted solely by man's intellectual curiosity, have not only enlarged man's understanding of himself and of the world around him, but have also shown a surprising capacity for being useful.

In my subject of scientific radio the whole earth itself is our laboratory, so that you can well understand the need for international collaboration. Fortunately, under the auspices of the International Scientific Radio Union, such collaboration has been forthcoming in full and generous measure. Next year the Union hopes to hold its 8th General Assembly in this beautiful city of Stockholm on the invitation of the Swedish National Radio Committee, whose President is Dr. Håkan Sterky.

It seems to me that we must recognize that the proper use of science is one of the most important challenges of the present day. And here I think the scientist has a twofold mission, not only of extending the frontiers of knowledge but also of interpreting his results to his fellow-men. For the use that can be made of the same scientific knowledge can be good or it can be evil. It is only in the heart of mankind that the distinction can be made. We have long realized that even the gift of radio, whereby nation can speak unto nation, can be abused and unworthily employed to generate hatred instead of to promote international friendship. Today the physicist, having unlocked the store of energy in the atom, demands that mankind shall choose the way in which his knowledge shall be used - whether it shall be used for the good or for the ruin of mankind.

It has been suggested in some quarters that the development of the benevolent uses of atomic energy can be separated clearly from the development of the atomic bomb, and that we can distinguish sharply between safe and dangerous activities in the atomic energy field. There can be no greater mistake. All activities can be safe. All activities can be dangerous. Mankind must decide which it shall be. The physicist, knowing better than anyone else the vital importance of the issues at stake, has already made known, in the clearest terms, what he feels the decision should be, and I, for one, am confident that the final decision of his fellow-men will be the same.

Finally, I would like to thank you all again for your charming hospitality - hospitality as graceful and gracious as Sweden herself.

# PATRICK M.S. BLACKETT
# 1948

## INTRODUCTION

Patrick Maynard Stuart Blackett was born on 18th November, 1897, the son of Arthur Stuart Blackett. He was originally trained as a regular officer for the Navy , and started his career as a naval cadet (1914), taking part, during the First World War, in the battles of Falkland Islands and Jutland. At the end of the war he resigned with the rank of Lieutenant, and took up studies of physics under Lord Rutherford at Cambridge.

After having taken his B.A. degree in 1921, he started research with cloud chambers which resulted, in 1924, in the first photographs of the transmutation of nitrogen into an oxygen isotope. In 1932, together with a young Italian scientist, G.P.S. Occhialini, he designed the counter-controlled cloud chamber, a brilliant invention by which they managed to make cosmic rays take their own photographs.

In the spring of 1933 they not only confirmed Anderson's discovery of the positive electron, but also demonstrated the existence of "showers" of positive and negative electrons, both in approximately equal numbers.

At the start of World War II, Blackett joined the Instrument Section of the Royal Aircraft Establishment. Early in 1940, he became Scientific Advisor to Air Marshall Joubert at Coastal Command, and started the analytical study of the anti U-boat war, building up a strong operational research group. In the same year he became Director of Naval Operational Research at the Admiralty, and continued the study of the anti U-boat war and other naval operations: later in 1940 he was appointed Scientific Advisor to General Pile, C.M.C., Anti-Aircraft Command, and built up an operational research group to study scientifically the various aspects of Staff work.

In 1945, at the end of the Second World War, work was resumed on cosmic ray investigations in the University of Manchester: in particular on the further study of cosmic ray particles by the counter-controlled cloud chamber in a strong magnetic field, built and used before the War. In 1947, Rochester and Butler, working in the laboratory, discovered the first two of what is now known to be a large family of the so-called strange particles.

In 1948 Blackett followed up speculations about the isotropy of cosmic rays and began speculating on the origin of the interstellar magnetic fields, and in so doing revived interest in some 30-year old speculations of Schuster and H. A. Wilson, and others, on the origin of the magnetic field of the earth and sun.

Professor Blackett was appointed Head of the Physics Department of the Imperial College of Science and Technology, London, in 1953 and retired in July, 1963. He is continuing at the Imperial College as Professor of Physics and Pro-Rector.

Blackett was awarded the Royal Medal by the Royal Society in 1940 and the American Medal for Merit, for operational research work in connection with the U-boat campaign, in 1946. He is the author of *Military and Political Consequences of Atomic Energy* (1948; revised edition 1949; American edition *Fear, War, and the Bomb,* 1949).

In 1924 he married Constanza Bayon; they have one son and one daughter.

## PRIZE ACCEPTANCE SPEECH

*Patrick M.S. Blackett's speech at the Nobel Banquet in Stockholm, December 10, 1948*

The honour which has been bestowed on me by the award by the Royal Academy of Sciences of Sweden of a Nobel Prize for Physics gives me a feeling of deep satisfaction and personal pride. However, I like to think of the award not only as a recognition of my own scientific work, but as a tribute to the vital school of European Experimental Physics in which I was trained. The fact that all four Nobel prizes this year, and so many others in recent years, have been awarded to Europeans is surely a striking tribute to the astonishing vitality in the Arts and Sciences of our irrepressible, colourful, turbulent but war-scarred Continent of Europe. In spite of two world wars in thirty years - eleven years of my own life have been spent in warfare, either as a fighting man or as a scientific analyst of tactics and strategy - in spite of the immense devastation of the continent, the stream of new scientific discovery and of literary creation is still in as full flood as ever before. Now we find ourselves surrounded by rumours and threats of a third world war - a war which, if it comes, will be made more terrible than the last through the wonderful discoveries in atomic physics of the last decades. It is a curious comment on the unexpected twists of human history to note that Alfred Nobel used a fortune made through the invention and manufacture of explosives to endow most generously prizes for outstanding achievement in the arts of peace - and by so doing has stimulated and encouraged the great stream of discovery in pure physics, which culminated in the overwhelming devastation of Hiroshima. From this rostrum in previous years have spoken to you, as Nobel Laureates, nearly all the great scientists whose work has made the atomic bomb possible - the Curies, Rutherford, Bohr, Aston, Joliot, Lawrence, Hahn, to name only a few.

Pure science has proved the most dangerous of pursuits. In the field of destruction the wise words of J. J. Thomson are as valid as in the arts of peace: "Applied science makes improvements; pure science makes revolutions."

The world today is facing the great problem of how to avoid a catastrophe made possible by the work of so many Nobel prizemen in Physics. It may be of interest to recall, however, that this is by no means the first time in history that mankind has felt the very basis of the established order threatened by the invention of a new weapon.

One such occasion was over 400 years ago. In 1494 Charles VIII of France crossed the Alps and rapidly destroyed, by means of artillery and Swiss infantry the military organisation of medieval Italy which was based on the fortified castle and the valor of the armoured knight. The poet Ariosto, contemporary of Machiavelli, wrote a poem dramatising the threat to the contemporary order. His hero, Orlando, embodiment of all the knightly virtues, meets an enemy with a firearm. When finally Orlando had triumphed, he took the offending weapon, sailed out into the ocean and plunged it into the sea exclaiming:

"Oh, Cursed device, Base Implement of Death
- - -
By Beelzebub's malicious art designed
To ruin all the race of human kind - - -
Here lie for ever in the abyss below!"

It might not be inappropriate to utter again these four centuries old words on the hoped for future occasion when the United Nations finally consign the world's store of atomic bombs to the depths of the ocean.

It is impossible to put the clock back - Machiavelli in his day could not stop the technological development which produced fire-arms - nor could Alfred Nobel stop those that followed his discovery of dynamite - nor can we stop the development of atomic energy. Technological progress and pure science are but different facets of the same growing mastery by man over the force of nature. It is our task as scientists and citizens to ensure that these forces are used for the good of man and not for their destruction.

# CECIL POWELL
# 1950

## INTRODUCTION

Cecil Frank Powell was born on December 5th, 1903, at Tonbridge, Kent, where his father, Frank Powell, was one of a family of gunsmiths who had long practised the trade in the town.

He attended a local elementary school and won a scholarship, at the age of eleven, to Judd School, Tonbridge. From there he won open scholarships to Sidney Sussex College, Cambridge, where he graduated with First Class Honours in the Natural Science Tripos (1924-1925).

As a postgraduate student, Powell worked in the Cavendish Laboratory under C.T.R. Wilson and Lord Rutherford until 1927 when he gained his Ph.D. and moved to the University of Bristol as Research Assistant to A.M. Tyndall in the H.H. Wills Physical Laboratory. He was eventually appointed lecturer, then reader and, in 1936, he visited the West Indies as seismologist of an expedition investigating volcanic activity. He returned to Bristol in the following year and in 1948 he was established as Melville Wills Professor of Physics.

Powell was Director of a European expedition for making high-altitude balloon flights in Sardinia (1952) and in the Po Valley (1954, 1955, and 1957).

His first researches at the Cavendish Laboratory concerned condensation phenomena and it led indirectly to an explanation of the anomalously high rate of discharge of steam through nozzles.

In 1938, he undertook experiments in cosmic radiation and employed methods of directly recording the tracks of the particles in photographic emulsions and, when the Cockcroft machine came into operation, he employed similar methods for determining the energy of neutrons, that is, by observing the tracks of the recoiling protons.

This development led him to a study of the scattering and disintegration processes produced by a beam of high-energy deuterons and he later returned, with the development of photographic emulsions of increased sensitivity, to experiments on cosmic radiation: in 1947 heavy mesons were discovered and many of their more important properties established.

Powell has contributed numerous papers to learned societies on the discharge of electricity in gases, and on the development of photographic methods in nuclear physics. He is a co-author of *Nuclear Physics in Photographs* (1947) and *The Study of Elementary Particles by the Photographic Method* (1959).

Prof. Powell was elected Fellow of the Royal Society in 1949: he was awarded the Hughes Medal in the same year and the Royal Medal in 1961. He has received honorary Doctor of Science degrees from the Universities of Dublin, Bordeaux and Warsaw, and he is a Foreign Member of the Academy of Sciences of the U.S.S.R. He was Vernon Boys Prizeman and Honorary Fellow of the Physical Society (1947), and he served on the Scientific Policy Committee of the European Organization for Nuclear Research (Geneva, 1961).

From Nobel Lectures, Physics 1942-1962, Elsevier Publishing Company, Amsterdam, 1964.

Cecil Powell died on August 9, 1969.

## PRIZE ACCEPTANCE SPEECH

*Cecil Powell's speech at the Nobel Banquet in Stockholm, December 10, 1950*

*Ladies and Gentlemen,*

Those placed in the position which I now occupy, commonly feel concern about their worthiness to receive the great honour which has been done them. How much more must this be so in my own case for I am conscious not only of the great names and achievements of those who have preceded me, but also of the living presence of many of my masters and teachers.

I am the fortunate representative of a group of many scientists, drawn from more than 20 nations, who have worked together in great harmony in Bristol in contributing to the development of a new tool in nuclear physics - a new method of making manifest the tracks of atomic particles in their passage through matter. Any device in science is a window on to nature, and each new window contributes to the breadth of our view. The particular features of the photographic method of detecting atomic particles enabled us to establish the existence of transient forms of matter which had escaped recognition by other methods.

In the course of this work, my colleagues and I have been deeply impressed by the powerful constructive forces which are set free when the representatives of many national traditions work harmoniously together for a common purpose. Within the limits of a single laboratory, we have experienced the invigorating effects of that international collaboration which is the life blood of the sciences in general. And this experience has given us some small insight into the tremendous advances which will become possible for humanity when that vision of a peaceful world and the fraternity of nations, which has animated men of good will since the beginning of history, has been made a reality. Make it so we shall because we must, and then we shall surely go out and conquer the universe.

In all our work, my colleagues and I have received inspiration even when we were least conscious of it, from those great aims of natural philosophy which were embodied in the doctrine of Utility and Progress, so clearly enunciated by my great country-man Francis Bacon; from that philanthropia, that love of humanity, which asserts that nothing is too trivial for the attention of the wisest which is capable of giving pleasure or pain to the meanest. These are the same aims which animated those who formulated the Code of Statutes of the Nobel Foundation. They are our most precious heritage; the source of our moral prestige without which we tend to become merely clever and lacking in humanity. May they ever be cherished so that we may all become, in Bacon's own words, the benefactors indeed of the human race, the propagators of man's empire over the universe, the champions of liberty and the conquerors and subduers of necessities.

Permit me to thank you for the great honour you have done me; for myself since you allow me to think that I have made some small contribution to that great scientific tradition in which I have been fostered, and which is part of the glory of my country; for my family, in giving us a most memorable experience on which we shall look back with great pleasure all our lives; and for my colleagues, because, in honouring me, you honour them also.

# E. M. PURCELL
## 1952

### INTRODUCTION

Edward Mills Purcell was born in Taylorville, Illinois, U.S.A., on August 30, 1912. His parents, Edward A. Purcell and Mary Elizabeth Mills, were both natives of Illinois. He was educated in the public schools in Taylorville and in Mattoon, Illinois, and in 1929 entered Purdue University in Indiana. He graduated from Purdue in electrical engineering in 1933.

His interest had already turned to physics, and through the kindness of Professor K. Lark-Horovitz he was enabled, while an undergraduate, to take part in experimental research in electron diffraction. As an Exchange Student of the Institute of International Education, he spent one year at the Technische Hochschule, Karlsruhe, Germany, where he studied under Professor W. Weizel. He returned to the United States in 1934 to enter Harvard University, where he received the Ph.D. degree in 1938. After serving two years as instructor in physics at Harvard, he joined the Radiation Laboratory, Massachusetts Institute of Technology, which was organized in 1940 for military research and development of microwave radar. He became Head of the Fundamental Developments Group in the Radiation Laboratory, which was concerned with the exploration of new frequency bands and the development of new microwave techniques. This experience turned out to be very valuable. Perhaps equally influential in his subsequent scientific work was the association at this time with a number of physicists, among them I.I. Rabi, with a continuing interest in the study of molecular and nuclear properties by radio methods.

The discovery of nuclear magnetic resonance absorption was made just after the end of the War, and at about that time Purcell returned to Harvard as Associate Professor of Physics. He became Professor of Physics in 1949; his present title is Gerhard Gade University Professor. He has continued to work in the field of nuclear magnetism, with particular interest in relaxation phenomena, related problems of molecular structure, measurement of atomic constants, and nuclear magnetic behaviour at low temperatures. He has made some contribution to the subject of radioastronomy.

He is a Fellow of the American Physical Society, a member of the National Academy of Sciences, of the American Academy of Arts and Sciences, and of the President's Science Advisory Committee under President Eisenhower from 1957-1960 and under President Kennedy as from 1960.

In 1937, Purcell married Beth C. Busser. They have two sons, Dennis and Frank.

*E.M. Purcell died on March 7, 1997.*

## PRIZE ACCEPTANCE SPEECH

*E. M. Purcell's speech at the Nobel Banquet in Stockholm, December 10, 1952*

*Your Majesties, Your Royal Highnesses, Ladies and gentlemen,*

The Nobel Prize, so long regarded in our science as the highest reward a man's work can earn, must bring to its recipient a most solemn sense of his debt to his fellow scientists and those of the past. You may be sure that Professor Bloch and I share alike in this feeling. It has been expressed more eloquently by others in this place. In these few words, I want to mention another result of our work, one that has deeply gratified us both. It is the fact that our particular field of research, growing since the war, has played some small part in renewing the bonds with laboratories in many countries. I think first of three great laboratories on this side of the Atlantic, the Kamerlingh Onnes Laboratory at Leiden, the Clarendon Laboratory at Oxford, and the Nobel Institute for Physics here in

Stockholm, with its illustrious tradition of elegant and precise experiment. Progress in the understanding of nuclear magnetism, and in its applications, owes very much to the work in these laboratories. But there are many other laboratories too, some as far away as Tokyo and Calcutta, where our scientific friends are working in nuclear magnetism. No walls of secrecy or suspicion divide us. On the contrary, free and friendy exchange of ideas has brought us close together. I wish only that these friends could share with us the warmth and kindness of your hospitality - for which, from Professor Bloch and myself, our very sincere thanks.

# MAX BORN
## 1954

### INTRODUCTION

Max Born was born in Breslau on the 11th December, 1882, to Professor Gustav Born, anatomist and embryologist, and his wife Margarete, *née* Kauffmann, who was a member of a Silesian family of industrialists. An appointment as professor to assist Max Planck at Berlin University came to Born in 1915 but he had to join the German Armed Forces. In a scientific office of the army he worked on the theory of sound ranging.

At the conclusion of the First World War, in 1919, Born was appointed Professor at the University of Frankfurt-on-Main, where a laboratory was put at his disposal. His assistant was Otto Stern, and the first of the latter's well-known experiments, which later were rewarded with a Nobel Prize, originated there.

Max Born went to Göttingen as Professor in 1921, at the same time as James Franck, and he remained there for twelve years, interrupted only by a trip to America in 1925. During the years 1925 and 1926 he published, with Heisenberg and Jordan, investigations on the principles of quantum mechanics (matrix mechanics) and soon after this, his own studies on the statistical interpretation of quantum mechanics.

As were so many other German scientists, he was forced to emigrate in 1933 and was invited to Cambridge, where he taught for three years as Stokes Lecturer.

During the winter of 1935-1936 Born spent six months in Bangalore at the Indian Institute of Science, where he worked with Sir C.V. Raman and his pupils. In 1936 he was appointed

Tait Professor of Natural Philosophy in Edinburgh, where he worked until his retirement in 1953.

Max Born has been awarded fellowships of many academies - Göttingen, Moscow, Berlin, Bangalore, Bucharest, Edinburgh, London, Lima, Dublin, Copenhagen, Stockholm, Washington, and Boston, and he has received honorary doctorates from Bristol, Bordeaux, Oxford, Freiburg/Breisgau, Edinburgh, Oslo, Brussels Universities, Humboldt University Berlin, and Technical University Stuttgart. In 1953 he was made honorary citizen of the town of Göttingen and a year later was granted the Nobel Prize for Physics. He was awarded the Grand Cross of Merit with Star of the Order of Merit of the German Federal Republic in 1959.

*Max Born died on January 5, 1970.*

## PRIZE ACCEPTANCE SPEECH

*Max Born's speech at the Nobel Banquet in Stockholm, December 10, 1954*

*Your Majesties, Your Royal Highnesses, Ladies and Gentlemen.*

When the work of a scientist is regarded by the Royal Swedish Academy of Science worth of the Nobel Prize, the highest honour open to a scholar, he will sense not only the deepest gratitude for this distinction but also a feeling of indebtedness to all those who have gone before and beside him. This feeling of all working together in the same direction is one of the most rewarding experiences of a scientist.

We are a great fellowship, men of all nations seeking after the truth. It is my greatest hope that the modern trend to subjugate science to politics and to inhuman ends and to erect barriers of fear and suspicion around national groups of scientists will not continue. For it is against the spirit of scientific research, as the mind can grow and bear fruit only in freedom.

The work for which the Nobel Prize has been awarded to me is of a kind which has no immediate effect on human life and activity, but rather on human thinking. But indirectly it had a considerable influence not only in physics but in other fields of human endeavour.

This transformation of thinking in which I have taken part is however a real child of science, not of philosophy: it was not the result of speculation, but forced upon us by the observed properties of Nature.

The facts known up to the end of the 19th century seemed to indicate that the world was a perfect mechanism, an automaton, so that if its configuration were known at a given instant its future behaviour could be predicted with certainty. This deterministic view was still generally accepted when I was young. But then new facts were discovered, in the realm of atoms as well as in the stellar universe, facts which did not fit in the mechanistic frame.

The human mind is conservative, and the scientist makes no exception from this rule. He will accept a new theory only if it stands the trial of many experimental tests. It was Prof. Walther Bothe with whom I share the honour of the Physics Prize, who devised the most powerful method of experimenting in this field. His results were decisive. I think that the statistical interpretation of the laws of nature to which I have been able to contribute has stood the test; it is universally accepted today. A philosophy in which the notions of chance and freedom are fundamental seems to me preferable to the almost inhuman determinism of the previous epoch - but that is no scientific argument.

The Royal Swedish Academy of Science has, by awarding to me the Nobel Prize for Physics, expressed the opinion that the ideas for which I have worked have been proved of value for the experimental scientist as well as for the theoretician. This is a great source of satisfaction to me.

My wife and I have been in this beautiful and hospitable country once before, on our honeymoon, a young and inconspicuous couple. We spent an unforgettable fortnight in the Cavaliershouse at Drottningholm. How little did we expect then, that after more than 40 years we should return under circumstances so entirely changed. My colleague Professor Bothe is unfortunately prevented by illness to be present. I deeply regret his absence and you all will share my good wishes for his speedy recovery.

May I express my sincerest gratitude for the great honour conferred upon me and for the very kind hospitality offered to my wife and myself, and to Prof. Bothe's children.

# POLYKARP KUSCH
## 1955

### INTRODUCTION

German-American physicist who, with Willis E. Lamb, Jr., was awarded the Nobel Prize for Physics in 1955 for his accurate determination that the magnetic moment of the electron is greater than its theoretical value, thus leading to reconsidera-tion of and innovations in quantum electrodyna-mics.

Kusch was brought to the United States in 1912 and became a citizen in 1922. In 1937, at Columbia University, he worked with the physicist Isidor I. Rabi on studies of the effects of magnetic fields on beams of atoms. He spent the wartime years in research on radar and returned to Columbia in 1946 as professor of physics, a position he held until 1972. Among other posts held by Kusch at Columbia were department chairman (1949–52, 1960–63), director of the radiation laboratory (1952–60), and academic vice president and provost (1969–72). In 1972 he took a position as professor at the University of Texas, Dallas, where he remained until his retirement in 1982.

In 1947, through precise atomic beam studies, Kusch demonstrated that the magnetic properties of the electron were not in agreement with existing theories. Subsequently, he made accurate measurements of the magnetic moment of the electron and its behaviour in hydrogen. In work characterized by great accuracy and reliability, he measured numerous atomic, molecular, and nuclear properties by radio-frequency beam techniques.

## PRIZE ACCEPTANCE SPEECH

*Polykarp Kusch' speech at the Nobel Banquet in Stockholm, December 10, 1955*

*Your Majesties, Your Royal Highnesses, Ladies and Gentlemen,*

No previous experience in life has given me the same sense of humility as the present one. This feeling is inevitable in view of the many illustrious names which adorn the roll of those whom the Swedish Academy of Science has honored through the award of the Nobel Prize. I am deeply conscious of and grateful for the honor bestowed upon me by the Swedish Academy in adding my name to the list of those who have received the Nobel Prize in Physics.

The increase of scientific knowledge lies not only in the occasional milestones of science, but in the efforts of the very large body of men who with love and devotion observe and study nature. No single achievement in science is possible without the painstaking work of the many hundreds who have built the foundation on which all new work is based. To these men I pay my homage.

Scientific experimentation is a complex procedure. It would be an impossible task to perform a meticulous experiment without the aid and help of the technicians, the machinists, the glassblowers and others. These men have been infected by the spirit of science, even if untrained in science and perform their work with skill and enthusiasm. It is to the generations of such unsung heroes that I also pay my tribute.

***Polykarp Kusch' Address to the University Students on the Evening of December 10, 1956***

First of all, let me thank you, on behalf of the Nobel Laureates of 1955, for your beautiful songs and your challenging words. In seeing you before me, I am again impressed by the certain knowledge that the future of truth and beauty as described by science and by the arts as well lies in your hands. The destiny of our society is yours to make and you have a vastly greater importance to the world than we do.

We live, I think, in the century of science and, perhaps, even in the century of physics. Science is the greatest creative impulse of our time. It dominates the intellectual scene and forms our lives, not only in the material things which it has given us, but also in that it guides our spirit. Science shows us truth and beauty and fills each day with a fresh wonder of the exquisite order which governs our world. I count myself fortunate to be able to participate in the life of science in this era. I feel, sometimes, as the renaissance man must have felt in finding new riches at every point and in the certainty that unexplored areas of knowledge and experience await at every turn. Those of us who have today been honored through the award of the Nobel Prize in the sciences envy those of you who are about to embark on a career in science. You have a world of unimaginable richness before you and we wish you well as you embark on your adventure of exploration.

The knowledge and understanding of the world which science gives us and the magnificent opportunity which it extends to us to control and use the world for the extension of our pleasure in it has never been greater than it now is. If, on occasion, the knowledge brought by science leads to an unhappy end, this is not to the discredit of science but is rather an indication of an imperfect ability to use wisely the gifts placed within our hands. To study man and his relationship with other men and the society in which he lives is the purpose of many of you. Indeed science alone may perhaps be sterile when pursued without an understanding of the world in which scientific knowledge is created and in which the fruits of science are used. To those of you who study history, economics, sociology, literature and language I present the challenge of the utilization of the enormous resources in our grasp to the problem of creating a genuinely good life for yourselves and your children. It is only through the combined efforts of all men of intelligence and understanding that this may be achieved.

Gentlemen! Every private carries in his knapsack a Marshall's baton. Go to it, with our best wishes!

# EUGENE WIGNER
## 1963

### INTRODUCTION

Eugene Paul Wigner, born in Budapest, Hungary, on November 17, 1902, naturalized a citizen of the United States on January 8, 1937, has been since 1938 Thomas D. Jones Professor of Mathematical Physics at Princeton University - he retired in 1971. His formal education was acquired in Europe; he obtained the Dr. Ing. degree at the Technische Hochschule Berlin.

Married in 1941 to Mary Annette Wheeler, he is the father of two children, David and Martha. His son, David, is teaching mathematics at the University of California in Berkeley. His daughter, Martha, is with the Chicago area transportation system, an organization endeavoring to improve the internal transportation system of that city. Dr.Wigner worked on the Manhattan Project at the University of Chicago during World War II, from 1942 to 1945, and in 1946-1947 became Director of Research and Development at Clinton Laboratories. Official recognition of his work in nuclear research includes the U. S. Medal for Merit, presented in 1946; the Enrico Fermi Prize (U.S.A.E.C.) awarded in 1958; and the Atoms for Peace Award, in 1960.

Dr. Wigner holds the Medal of the Franklin Society, the Max Planck Medal of the German Physical Society, the George Washington Award of the American-Hungarian Studies Foundation (1964), the Semmelweiss Medal of the American-Hungarian Medical Association (1965), and the National Medal of Science (1969).

He has received honorary degrees from the University of Wisconsin, Washington University, Case Institute, University of Alberta (Canada), University of Chicago, Colby College, University of Pennsylvania, Yeshiva University, Thiel College, Notre Dame University, Technische Universität Berlin, Swarthmore College, Université de Louvain, Université de Liège, University of Illinois, Seton Hall, Catholic University and The Rockefeller University.

He is a past vice- president and president of the American Physical Society, of which he remains a member. He is a past member of the board of directors of the American Nuclear Society and still a member; he holds memberships in the American Philosophical Society, the American Mathematical Society, the American Association of Physics Teachers, the National Academy of Science, the American Academy of Arts and Sciences, the Royal Netherlands Academy of Sciences and Letters, the American Association for the Advancement of Science, the Austrian Academy of Sciences and foreign member of the Royal Society of Great Brittain.

He was a member of the General Advisory Committee to the U.S. Atomic Energy Commission from 1952-1957, was reappointed to this committee in 1959 and served on it until 1964.

Eugene Wigner died on January 1, 1995.

## PRIZE ACCEPTANCE SPEECH

*Eugene Wigner's speech at the Nobel Banquet in Stockholm, December 10, 1963*

I wish to thank first in the names of Drs. Maria Goeppert Mayer and Jensen, as well as in my own name, for the honor we received and for the beautiful celebration, for the truly heart-warming festivities, which we all enjoyed. We are all deeply grateful. However, new gratitude should never efface old ones and I wish to say at this occasion a few words on a subject about which we think little when young but which we appreciate increasingly when we reflect on our intellectual development. I mean our indebtedness to our teachers.

Man's knowledge has become man's knowledge rather than individual knowledge because he has developed codes in which sound signals correspond to objects and actions and he can learn one of these codes early in life in some mysterious way. Hence, people can communicate their knowledge and teach each other. Much of what we know, and most of the science which we know, was taught to us in this way. This process may be called manifest teaching-learning. Much can be said about this, in fact much has been said about it, but this is not my concern this evening.

What I wish to draw attention to is how much of our interest in science, and how much of our attitude toward science, we owe to our teachers. My own history begins in the high-school in Hungary where my mathematics teacher, Ratz, gave me books to read and evoked in me a sense for the beauty of his subject. I can not mention all to whom I am indebted but I do wish to mention the inspiration received from Polanyi. He taught me, among other things, that science begins when a body of phenomena is available which shows some coherence and regularities, that science consists in assimilating these regularities and in creating concepts which permit expressing these regularities in a natural way. He also taught me that it is this method of science rather than the concepts themselves (such as energy) which should be applied to other fields of learning.

We have not only teachers who are older than we, we learn also from contemporaries and younger colleagues. The contemporary from whom I learned most - in fact immensely much - was von Neumann but that was mostly mathematics. In leadership a young man at that time, Ray Herb, was my tutor. My scientific attitudes were greatly influenced also by students - some of whom had a more mature outlook than I. Perhaps I better not mention names lest they ask for a return of the tuition fee. To all of them I am deeply grateful, as we are to you for all that we have experienced today.

# CHARLES H. TOWNES
## 1964

### INTRODUCTION

Charles Hard Townes was born in Greenville, South Carolina, on July 28, 1915, the son of Henry Keith Townes, an attorney, and Ellen (Hard) Townes. He attended the Greenville public schools and then Furman University in Greenville, where he completed the requirements for the Bachelor of Science degree in Physics and the Bachelor of Arts degree in Modern Languages, graduating *summa cum laude* in 1935, at the age of 19.

Townes completed work for the Master of Arts degree in Physics at Duke University in 1936, and then entered graduate school at the California Institute of Technology, where he received the Ph.D. degree in 1939 with a thesis on isotope separation and nuclear spins.

At Columbia University, where he was appointed to the faculty in 1948, he continued research in microwave physics, particularly studying the interactions between microwaves and molecules, and using microwave spectra for the study of the structure of molecules, atoms, and nuclei. In 1951, Dr. Townes conceived the idea of the maser, and a few months later he and his associates began working on a device using ammonia gas as the active medium.

In early 1954, the first amplification and generation of electromagnetic waves by stimulated emission were obtained. In 1958, Dr. Townes and his brother-in-law, Dr. A.L. Schawlow, for some time a professor at Stanford University but now deceased, showed theoretically that masers could be made to operate in the optical and infrared region and proposed how this could be accomplished in particular systems.

From 1959 to 1961, he was on leave of absence from Columbia University to serve as Vice President and Director of Research of the Institute for Defense Analyses in Washington, D.C., a nonprofit organization which advised the U.S. government and was operated by eleven universities.

In 1966, he became Institute Professor at M.I.T., and later in the same year resigned from the position of Provost in order to return to more intensive research, particularly in the fields of quantum electronics and astronomy. He was appointed University Professor at the University of California in 1967.

In addition to the Nobel Prize, Townes has received the Templeton Prize, for contributions to the understanding of religion, and a number of other prizes as well as 27 honorary degrees from various universities.

Dr. Townes has served on a number of scientific committees advising governmental agencies and has been active in professional societies. This includes being a member, and vice chairman, of the Science Advisory Committee to the President of the U.S., Chairman of the Advisory Committee for the first human landing on the moon, and chairman of the Defense Department's Committee on the MX missile. He also served on the boards of General Motors and of the Perkins Elmer Corporations.

Dr. Townes and his wife (the former Frances H. Brown; they married in 1941) live at 1988 San Antonio Avenue, Berkeley, California. They have four daughters, Linda Rosenwein, Ellen Anderson, Carla Kessler, and Holly Townes.

## PRIZE ACCEPTANCE SPEECH

*Charles H. Townes' speech at the Nobel Banquet in Stockholm, December 10, 1964*

*Your Majesties, Your Royal Highnesses, Your Excellences, Ladies and Gentlemen:*

The wisdom of the Swedish people, the warm interest of Sweden's Royal Family and the dedication of its Academies have made much more than a reality of Alfred Nobel's magnificent concept. They have endowed the Nobel Prize with an aura which has inspired intellectual and creative work everywhere. They brought a special affection for Sweden and its ideals. And they have made this occasion to the highest point in the public part of any scientist's career. I am, of course, deeply grateful to you and will treasure this connection with Sweden.

But there are also other things for which I am grateful, which may be a little less obvious on this occasion when a few individuals are singled out for high honour. There is some truth to the idea that in the fields of science individual contributions of great significance are possible. The development of science is basically a social phenomenon, dependent on hard work and mutual support of many scientists and on the societies in which they live. Scientists do, as we have heard, stand on the shoulders of giants from the past. And we who have been honoured here today have also depended heavily on the work of many others - our colleagues, some of whom are as worthy of being here as we are, some of whom have carried out fascinating and essential exploration of a slightly less spectacular nature, some of whom have done necessary work with devotion and courage on problems which today seem not to have been very fruitful. To all of these I am grateful.

The worldwide character of scientific community and much of this mutual support in science is well illustrated by the Laureates here tonight. No one can be an intimate part of a scientific effort without being appreciative of the exciting and cumulative effects of this broad cooperation and of the coherence - if I may use a term familiar in my own field: the masers - of the many individual contributions to science. Nor can any scientist be an intimate part of his world, without wondering if somehow other more difficult aspects of human affairs can experience more strongly these coherent and cumulative effects, if a larger portion of human efforts can be additive and mutually supporting. Our nature is of course more severely taxed in nonscientific fields, to clearly recognize overriding human goals and to work towards them with objectivity and sometimes at personal and national sacrifice when we no longer have hard experimental results to straighten us out, when we err a little too far. But the imposing edifice of science provides a challenging view of what can be achieved by the accumulation of many small efforts in a steady objective and dedicated search for truth.

Alfred Nobel really understood very well the necessary supra-natural character of the human enterprise. His representatives here, and Sweden as a nation, have carried out a noble and an extraordinary pursuit of this idea. For this we can all be grateful and we wish them well. There is, however, hard work ahead for all of us. And if we succeed in making appreciably more coherent our individual human effort, and in crossing a few thresholds, we have not attained so far, the results can be amazing. Thank you.

# RICHARD P. FEYNMAN
## 1965

### INTRODUCTION

Richard P. Feynman was born in New York City on the 11th May 1918. He studied at the Massachusetts Institute of Technology where he obtained his B.Sc. in 1939 and at Princeton University where he obtained his Ph.D. in 1942.

He was Research Assistant at Princeton (1940-1941), Professor of Theoretical Physics at Cornell University (1945-1950), Visiting Professor and thereafter appointed Professor of Theoretical Physics at the California Institute of Technology (1950-1959). At present he is Richard Chace Tolman Professor of Theoretical Physics at the California Institute of Technology.

Professor Feynman is a member of the American Physical Society, the American Association for the Advancement of Science; the National Academy of Science; in 1965 he was elected a foreign member of the Royal Society, London (Great Britain).

He holds the following awards: Albert Einstein Award (1954, Princeton); Einstein Award (Albert Einstein Award College of Medicine); Lawrence Award (1962).

Richard Feynman is married to Gweneth Howarth, they have a son, Carl Richard (born 22nd April 1961), and a daughter Michelle Catherine (born 13th August 1968).

*Richard P. Feynman died on February 15, 1988.*

# PRIZE ACCEPTANCE SPEECH

*Richard P. Feynman's speech at the Nobel Banquet in Stockholm, December 10, 1965*

*Your Majesty, Your Royal Highnesses, Ladies and Gentlemen.*

The work I have done has, already, been adequately rewarded and recognized.

Imagination reaches out repeatedly trying to achieve some higher level of understanding, until suddenly I find myself momentarily alone before one new corner of nature's pattern of beauty and true majesty revealed. That was my reward.

Then, having fashioned tools to make access easier to the new level, I see these tools used by other men straining their imaginations against further mysteries beyond. There, are my votes of recognition.

Then comes the prize, and a deluge of messages. Reports; of fathers turning excitedly with newspapers in hand to wives; of daughters running up and down the apartment house ringing neighbor's doorbells with news; victorious cries of "I told you so" by those having no technical knowledge - their successful prediction being based on faith alone; from friends, from relatives, from students, from former teachers, from scientific colleagues, from total strangers; formal commendations, silly jokes, parties, presents; a multitude of messages in a multitude of forms.

But, in each I saw the same two common elements. I saw in each, joy; and I saw affection (you see, whatever modesty I may have had has been completely swept away in recent days).

The prize was a signal to permit them to express, and me to learn about, their feelings. Each joy, though transient thrill, repeated in so many places amounts to a considerable sum of human happiness. And, each note of affection released thus one upon another has permitted me to realize a depth of love for my friends and acquaintances, which I had never felt so poignantly before.

For this, I thank Alfred Nobel and the many who worked so hard to carry out his wishes in this particular way.

And so, you Swedish people, with your honors, and your trumpets, and your king - forgive me. For I understand at last - such things provide entrance to the heart. Used by a wise and peaceful people they can generate good feeling, even love, among men, even in lands far beyond your own. For that lesson, I thank you. Tack!

# HANS BETHE
## 1967

### INTRODUCTION

Hans Albrecht Bethe was born in Strasbourg, Alsace-Lorraine, on July 2 1906. He attended the Gymnasium in Frankfurt from 1915 to 1924. He then studied at the University of Frankfurt for two years, and at Munich for two and one half years, taking his Ph. D. in theoretical physics with Professor Arnold Sommerfeld in July 1928. He then was an Instructor in physics at Frankfurt and at Stuttgart for one semester each. From fall 1929 to fall 1933 his headquarters were the University of Munich where he became Privatdozent in May 1930.

Bethe emigrated to England in October 1933 where he held a temporary position as Lecturer at the University of Manchester for the year 1933-1934, and a fellowship at the University of Bristol in the fall of 1934. In February 1935 he was appointed Assistant Professor at Cornell University, Ithaca, N. Y. U.S.A., then promoted to Professor in the summer of 1937. He has stayed there ever since, except for sabbatical leaves and for an absence during World War II.

Bethe's main work is concerned with the theory of atomic nuclei. Together with Peierls, he developed a theory of the deuteron in 1934 which he extended in 1949. He resolved some contradictions in the nuclear mass scale in 1935. He studied the theory of nuclear reactions in 1935-1938, predicting many reaction cross sections. In connection with this work, he developed Bohr's theory of the compound nucleus in a more quantitative fashion.

His work on nuclear reactions led Bethe to the discovery of the reactions which supply the energy in the stars. The most important nuclear reaction in the brilliant stars is the carbon-nitrogen cycle, while the sun and fainter stars use mostly the proton-proton reaction. Bethe's main achievement in this connection was the exclusion of other possible nuclear reactions. The Nobel Prize was given for this work, as well as his work on nuclear reactions in general.

In 1955 Bethe returned to the theory of nuclei, emphasizing a different phase. He has worked since then on the theory of nuclear matter whose aim it is to explain the properties of atomic nuclei in terms of the forces acting between nucleons.

Bethe also did some work on solid-state theory. He discussed the splitting of atomic energy levels when an atom is inserted into a crystal, he did some work on the theory of metals, and especially he developed a theory of the order and disorder in alloys.

In 1947, Bethe was the first to explain the Lamb-shift in the hydrogen spectrum, and he thus laid the foundation for the modern development of quantum electrodynamics. Later on, he worked with a large number of collaborators on the scattering of pi mesons and on their production by electromagnetic radiation.

Bethe is married to the daughter of P.P. Ewald, the well-known X-ray physicist. They have two children, Henry and Monica.

*Hans Bethe died on March 6, 2005.*

## PRIZE ACCEPTANCE SPEECH

*Hans Bethe's speech at the Nobel Banquet in Stockholm, December 10, 1967*

*Your Majesty, Your Royal Highnesses, Ladies and Gentlemen.*

I am deeply grateful to you for bestowing on me the Nobel Prize. For many decades this Prize has been regarded as the highest honor which can be awarded to a scientist. I feel quite humble comparing myself with many of my predecessors who have made great and fundamental discoveries. You have given me the Prize I believe for a lifetime of quiet work in physics rather than for any spectacular single contribution. I am very proud and very happy with this distinction.

One of the happiest parts has been the response of so many of my friends. I have received many hundreds of letters and telegrams of congratulations, and it seems to me that all of them really shared my joy about the Prize. Many more, I suppose, were happy about it without telling me directly. And I suppose that the same is true for every Nobel Prize; it is enjoyed not only by the recipient, but by many others.

Mr. Nobel, when he started the Nobel Prize, can hardly have known how many people he would make happy. He probably thought of the future prize winners, and that he would make their scientific life easier and more pleasant. But he probably did not imagine that with each prize he would bring happiness to hundreds of others as well.

In our country we often try to persuade rich men to leave their money to universities. This is certainly a good cause and, if the same custom applies here in Sweden, Nobel might well have left his fortune to for instance the University of Uppsala. This would have been of great benefit to that university, and perhaps especially to the pursuit of science there. However, these benefits could not remotely compare to those which Nobel achieved by establishing the Prizes. They have stimulated science all over the world; they have stimulated governments and universities to give more support to science; and they have added prestige to science in the eyes of young students.

That the Prizes have acquired this prestige is of course mostly the merit of the Swedish Royal Academy. I have sat on committees to select the recipients for lesser prizes, and I know what a hard job it is. It must be enormously more troublesome for the Nobel Prizes. I have always admired the selections they have made, and I am not saying this because I am one of the lucky ones.

We are all unhappy that nobody today will receive the Peace Prize. Unfortunately it is not surprising in the present world that the Norwegian Parliament could not find anybody who has contributed sufficiently to peace to merit the Prize. I believe I express the hope of all of us that a Peace Prize can be given next year.

# LUIS ALVAREZ
## 1968

### INTRODUCTION

Luis W. Alvarez was born in San Francisco, Calif., on June 13, 1911. He received his B.Sc. from the University of Chicago in 1932, a M.Sc. in 1934, and his Ph.D. in 1936. Dr. Alvarez joined the Radiation Laboratory of the University of California, where he is now a professor, as a research fellow in 1936. He was on leave at the Radiation Laboratory of the Massachusetts Institute of Technology from 1940 to 1943, at the Metallurgical Laboratory of the University of Chicago in 1943-1944, and at the Los Alamos Laboratory of the Manhattan District from 1944.

Dr. Alvarez is responsible for the design and construction of the Berkeley 40-foot proton linear accelerator, which was completed in 1947. In 1951 he published the first suggestion for charge exchange acceleration that quickly led to the development of the "Tandem Van de Graaf accelerator". Since that time, he has engaged in high-energy physics, using the 6 billion electron volt Bevatron at the University of California Radiation Laboratory. His main efforts have been concentrated on the development and use of large liquid hydrogen bubble chambers, and on the development of high-speed devices to measure and analyze the millions of photographs produced each year by the bubble-chamber complex. The net result of this work has been the discovery by Dr. Alvarez' research group, of a large number of previously unknown efundamental particle resonances.. Since 1967 Dr. Alvarez has devoted most of this time to the study of cosmic rays, using balloons and superconducting magnets.

Professor Alvarez is a member of the following societies: National Academy of Sciences, American Philosophical Society, American Physical Society (President 1969), American Academy of Arts and Sciences, and National Academy of Engineering. In 1946 he was awarded the Collier Trophy by the National Aeronautical Association for the development of Ground - Controlled Approach. In 1953 he was awarded the John Scott Medaland Prize, by the city of Philadelphia, for the same work. In 1947 he was awarded the Medal for Merit. In 1960 he was named "California Scientist of the Year" for his research work on high-energy physics. In 1961 he was awarded the Einstein Medal for his contribution to the physical sciences. In 1963 he was awarded the Pioneer Award of the AIEEE; in 1964 he was awarded the National Medal of Science for contributions to high-energy physics, and in 1965 he received the Michelson Award. He has received the following honorary de grees: Sc.D., University of Chicago, 1967; Sc.D., Carnegie-Mellon University, 1968; Sc.D., Kenyon College, 1969.

*Luis Alvarez died on September 1, 1988.* –

## PRIZE ACCEPTANCE SPEECH

*Luis Alvarez' speech at the Nobel Banquet in Stockholm, December 10, 1968*

*Your Majesty. Your Royal Highnesses, your Excellencies, Ladies and Gentlemen:*

I learned much of the physics I know from two men who preceded me to this banquet table - Arthur Compton and Ernest Lawrence. Because Ernest Lawrence's award came in the war years, I had the unusual opportunity of attending his Nobel Prize presentation ceremony. The Swedish Ambassador to our country came to California to represent his King. I remember the pleasure and satisfaction I had in hearing my friend and Laboratory director mention some of my own work, that had contributed in small measure to the broad picture of Ernest Lawrence's great influence on modern physics.

One indicator of Ernest Lawrence's influence is the fact that I am the eighth member of his laboratory staff to receive the highest award that can come to a scientist - the Nobel Prize. I am deeply grateful to the Royal Swedish Academy of Science for judging me worthy to be associated in this way with my esteemed colleagues, and with the other distinguished physicists who have sat at this table in years past.

I am particularly happy that a number of my young colleagues are here tonight to share with me the great recognition that our joint efforts over the years has just been accorded. We all appreciate that the Prize must be given to a person, rather than to a group, but we are all honest enough with each other to understand just how much of a group effort our work really was. I was afraid that this knowledge might be a sort of private secret between us, so I was delighted to hear my old friend Sten von Friesen refer this afternoon to "a whole series of discoveries made by Alvarez' group in Berkeley". That is the way I remember it, and because of my previous experience at the ceremony in Berkeley almost thirty years ago, I feel particularly close to my colleagues assembled here tonight.

In addition to my teachers and my colleagues, I would like to mention one other person who shares equally in the responsibility for my presence here tonight. Janet Landis came to work in my group in the summer of 1957 when our first bubble-chamber was churning out its earliest pictures. She scanned and measured the photographs, she operated the computer, and she later trained and supervised the people who did that work. Almost exactly ten years ago, she left the Laboratory to become my wife. Since then, she has rearranged our living room every Monday night to entertain forty of my young associates who arrive on schedule for our weekly seminar. She has provided the warmth and understanding that a scientist needs to tide him over the periods of frustration and despair that seem to be part of our way of life. I know it is an old Swedish custom that a man must Skål his wife at a banquet under penalty of dire consequences for failure. So with your permission, I will now Skål my Jan.

# ANTONY HEWISH
## 1974

### INTRODUCTION

British astrophysicist who won the Nobel Prize for Physics in 1974 for his discovery of pulsars (cosmic objects that emit extremely regular pulses of radio waves).

Hewish was educated at the University of Cambridge and in 1946 joined the radio astronomy group there led by Sir Martin Ryle. While directing a research project at the Mullard Radioastronomy Observatory at Cambridge in 1967, Hewish recognized the significance of an observation made by a graduate assistant, Jocelyn Bell.

He determined that the regularly patterned radio signals, or pulses, that Bell had detected were not caused by earthly interference or, as some speculated, by intelligent life forms trying to communicate with distant planets but rather were energy emissions from certain stars. For this work in identifying pulsars as a new class of stars, he was awarded jointly with Ryle the Nobel Prize for Physics in 1974, the first time the prize had been given for observational astronomy.

Hewish was professor of radio astronomy at the Cavendish Laboratory, Cambridge, from 1971 to 1989.

## PRIZE ACCEPTANCE SPEECH

*Antony Hewish's speech at the Nobel Banquet, December 10, 1974*

*Your Majesty, Your Royal Highnesses, Ladies and Gentlemen,*

The world of man lies midway in scale between the inner space of atoms and particles, and the outer space of stars and galaxies. The exploration of both these regions stretches our imagination to its limits.

In deciding to honour the field of Astrophysics the Nobel Foundation, and the Royal Academy of Sciences, have given great encouragement and delight to all astronomers who share with us this proud moment. Sir Martin Ryle and I know this well from the countless messages that we have received from all over the world.

There is, I think, some special benefit for mankind in the realm of astrophysics. It is impossible to witness the interplay of galaxies without a sense of wonder, and looking back at Earth we see it in its true perspective, a planet of great beauty, an undivided sphere. Let us try and keep this image always in our view.

# SUBRAMANYAN CHANDRASEKHAR
## 1983

### INTRODUCTION

Indian-born American astrophysicist who, with William A. Fowler, won the 1983 Nobel Prize for Physics for key discoveries that led to the currently accepted theory on the later evolutionary stages of massive stars.

Chandrasekhar was the nephew of Sir C. V. Raman, who won the Nobel Prize for Physics in 1930.

Chandrasekhar was educated at Presidency College, at the University of Madras, and at Trinity College, Cambridge. From 1933 to 1936 he held a position at Trinity.

By the early 1930s, scientists had concluded that, after converting all of their hydrogen to helium, stars lose energy and contract under the influence of their own gravity. These stars, known as white dwarf stars, contract to about the size of the Earth, and the electrons and nuclei of their constituent atoms are compressed to a state of extremely high density. Chandrasekhar determined what is known as the Chandrasekhar limit—that a star having a mass more than 1.44 times that of the Sun does not form a white dwarf but instead continues to collapse, blows off its gaseous envelope in a supernova explosion, and becomes a neutron star.

Chandrasekhar joined the staff of the University of Chicago, rising from assistant professor of astrophysics (1938) to Morton D. Hull distinguished service professor of astrophysics (1952), and became a U.S. citizen in 1953. He did important work on energy transfer by radiation in stellar atmospheres and convection on the solar surface. He also attempted to develop the mathematical theory of black holes, describing his work in *The Mathematical Theory of Black Holes* (1983).

Chandrasekhar was awarded the Gold Medal of the Royal Astronomical Society in 1953 and the Royal Medal of the Royal Society in 1962.

## PRIZE ACCEPTANCE SPEECH

*Subramanyan Chandrasekhar's speech at the Nobel Banquet, December 10, 1983*

*Your Majesties, Your Royal Highnesses, Ladies and Gentlemen,*

The award of a Nobel Prize carries with it so much distinction and the number of competing areas and discoveries are so many, that it must of necessity have a sobering effect on an individual who receives the Prize. For who will not be sobered by the realization that among the past Laureates there are some who have achieved a measure of insight into Nature that is far beyond the attainment of most? But I am grateful for the award since it is possible that it may provide a measure of encouragement to those, who like myself, have been motivated in their scientific pursuits, principally, for achieving personal perspectives, while wandering, mostly, in the lonely byways of Science. When I say personal perspectives, I have in mind the players in Virginia Woolf's *The Waves*:

There is a square; there is an oblong. The players take the square and place it upon the oblong. They place it very accurately; they make a perfect dwelling-place. Very little is left outside. The structure is now visible; what is inchoate is here stated; we are not so various or so mean; we have made oblongs and stood them upon squares. This is our triumph; this is our consolation.

May I be allowed to quote some further lines from a writer of a very different kind. They are from *Gijtanjali*, a poem by Rabindranath Tagore who was honoured on this same date exactly seventy years ago. I learnt the poem when I was a boy of twelve some sixty and more years ago; and the following lines have remained with me ever since:

Where the mind is without fear and the head is held high;Where knowledge is free; Where words come out from the depth of truth; Where tireless striving stretches its arms towards perfection; Where the clear stream of reason has not lost its way into the dreary desert sand of dead habit; into that haven of freedom, Let me awake.

May I, on behalf of my wife and myself, express our immense gratitude to the Nobel Foundation for this noble reception in this noble city?

# MARTIN L. PERL
## 1995

### INTRODUCTION

American physicist who received the 1995 Nobel Prize for Physics for discovering a subatomic particle that he named the tau, a massive lepton with a negative charge. The tau, which he found in the mid-1970s, was the first evidence of a third "generation" of fundamental particles, the existence of which proved essential for completing the so-called standard model of particle physics. Perl was jointly awarded the Nobel Prize with physicist Frederick Reines (*q.v.*), who discovered another subatomic particle, the neutrino, in the 1950s.

In 1948 Perl graduated from the Brooklyn Polytechnic Institute with a degree in chemical engineering. After working as a chemical engineer for two years, he studied nuclear physics at Columbia University (Ph.D., 1955). He was an instructor and associate professor at the University of Michigan (1955–63) before joining the faculty of Stanford University in 1963.

In 1966 Perl was part of a research team that made an unsuccessful attempt to discover new charged leptons by colliding electrons at the Stanford Linear Accelerator Center (SLAC). A new particle accelerator that began operation at SLAC in the early 1970s had the capacity to reach high energy levels that were previously inaccessible. With this new machine, Perl recorded frontal collisions between electrons and their antiparticles, positrons. In a series of experiments conducted between 1974 and 1977, he found that the collisions formed heavy leptons, later called tau particles, that decay in less than a trillionth of a second into neutrinos and either an electron or a muon. He also discovered the antitau, which decays into neutrinos and either a positron or an antimuon.

## PRIZE ACCEPTANCE SPEECH

*Martin L. Perl's speech at the Nobel Banquet, December 10, 1995*

*Your Majesties, Your Royal Highnesses, Ladies and Gentlemen,*

On behalf of my companion in the world of lepton physics, Frederick Reines, and myself I want to express our gratitude to the Royal Swedish Academy of Sciences and the Nobel Foundation for being honored for our discoveries in physics. It is a great pleasure for us to be here today, indeed it is a special pleasure because the physics world may not show much gratitude in the future for our work. Our discoveries may have brought up more problems than we solved. I will explain.

Before Frederick Reines and Clyde Cowan proved the physical existence of the neutrino it was possible to think of the neutrino as a vague sort of entity, perhaps not quite physical, perhaps only a mathematical concept. But their discovery forced the physics world to confront the question of what is the mass of the neutrino. If the mass is zero, how can a particle of zero mass carry information about its properties? If the neutrino mass is not zero, then what is its mass, and what law of physics fixes its mass? There have been many attempts to find the mass of the neutrino and such experiments continue. But still the mass has not been measured. Thus the discovery for which Frederick Reines is being honored today has raised more questions than he answered.

I must confess that my discovery of the tau lepton has left us with a similar situation. I began my research trying to find the connection between the electron and the muon, the two charged leptons which were known before 1975. Since my colleagues and I could not find the connection, I decided to look for an additional charged lepton, a heavier lepton, hoping that the heavier lepton would teach us about the connections between charged leptons. With the help of my colleagues, particularly Gary Feldman and Paul Tsai who are here tonight, the heavy lepton was found, and we called it the tau. Since this discovery a great deal of experimental work has been done on the tau lepton. And there has been a great deal of theoretical work, particularly by Haim Harari who is also here tonight. But none of us have been able to penetrate the secret of what is now a more complicated question. What is the connection between the electron, the muon, and the tau? Thus the discovery of the tau lepton also raised more questions than it answered.

Perhaps Frederick Reines and I are not working in the right directions, perhaps some young woman or some young man will point lepton physics in the right direction and will answer the multitude of questions we have raised.

# ZHORES I. ALFEROV
## 2000

### INTRODUCTION

*Zhores Ivanovich Alfyorov,* Soviet physicist who, with Herbert Kroemer and Jack S. Kilby, was awarded the Nobel Prize for Physics in 2000 for their work that laid the foundation for the modern era of computers and information technology.

Alferov received a doctorate in physics and mathematics from the A.F. Ioffe Physico-Technical Institute (1970); he became director of the institute in 1987. In the 1950s he began work to develop fast optoelectronic and microelectronic components made from semiconductor heterostructures. (While most computer chips and other semiconductor components were made from one kind of material, such as silicon, heterostructure semiconductors were made from layers of different materials.)

Using Kroemer's theory, which suggested that a heterostructure transistor was superior to a conventional transistor, Alferov and his research team developed the first practical heterostructure electronic device in 1966. They then pioneered electronic components made from heterostructures, including the first heterostructure laser, which both Alferov and Kroemer had proposed independently in 1963. Heterostructure solid-state lasers made possible fibre-optic communications, and heterostructure devices were later used in communications satellites, bar-code readers, cellular telephone communications, and other products.

## PRIZE ACCEPTANCE SPEECH

*Zhores I. Alferov's speech at the Nobel Banquet, December 10, 2000*

*Your Majesties, Your Royal Highnesses, Ladies and Gentlemen,*

Allow me first of all, on behalf of my colleagues Professor Herbert Kroemer and Dr. Jack Kilby and myself to express our deepest gratitude to the Royal Swedish Academy of Sciences for awarding us the most prestigious Prize in history - the Nobel Prize.

The Nobel Prize in Physics 2000, at the change of centuries, has a special meaning. The twentieth century was not only the century of wars and social explosions, it was the century of Physics and first of all quantum Physics. Positive progress of human kind (unfortunately not only positive) was linked with discoveries and development in this field of sciences.

As it was pointed out by a great physicist John Bardeen, only one who had two Nobel Prizes in Physics: "That science knows no national boundaries is an old story to scientists but is perhaps not as well appreciated by the general public".

Just after the World War II discovery of the transistor and laser-maser principles - became the roots of information technology of the XX-th century.

Invention of integrated circuits and creation of a new kind of materials - "Man-made crystals" -semiconductor heterostructures - led to the modern level of information and communication technology. The important consequences of that technological breakthrough caused an overhaul in social structure of society - that is what we call now the postindustrial or informational society.

As always, we have, of course, from scientific and technological discoveries and inventions not only positive, but also negative results. Electronic mass media - being very strong and powerful weapon, unfortunately sometimes gets into hands of dishonest and irresponsible people.

We should recall the words of a great thinker Francis Bacon - Knowledge is Power. But what is also very important:

The Power must be based on Knowledge.

At the time that we commenced our research on making the double heterostructure laser:

> Our purpose was both great and bright
> No more the dark! Let there be light
> So, to release eternal light
> We did the work all day and night
> And when could neither work nor think
> We had the Russian vodka drink
> And we must find, as years pass
> What Nature has in store for us
> Young Folk have come, results are new
> And to Physical Review
> My students' work is to be sent
> So our life will never end.

# RICCARDO GIACCONI
# 2002

## INTRODUCTION

Italian-born physicist who won the Nobel Prize for Physics in 2002 for his seminal discoveries of cosmic sources of X rays, which helped lay the foundations for the field of X-ray astronomy. Raymond Davis, Jr., and Koshiba Masatoshi also won a share of the award for their research on neutrinos.

Giacconi received a Ph.D. from the University of Milan in 1954. In 1959 he joined the research firm American Science and Engineering, and in 1973 he moved to the Harvard-Smithsonian Center for Astrophysics. He later directed the Space Telescope Science Institute (1981–93) and the European Southern Observatory (1993–99). In 1999 Giacconi became president of Associated Universities, Incorporated, which operates the National Radio Astronomy Observatory.

Giacconi began his award-winning work in X-ray astronomy in 1959, about a decade after astronomers had first detected X rays from the Sun. Because X rays emitted by cosmic objects are absorbed by the Earth's atmosphere, this radiation could be studied only after the development of sounding rockets that could carry X-ray detectors above most of the atmosphere for brief flights. Giacconi conducted a number of these rocket observations: the data led to the detection of intense X rays from sources outside the solar system, including the star Scorpius X-1 and the Crab Nebula supernova remnant.

Giacconi's achievements piqued the interest of other scientists in the nascent field of X-ray astronomy, but their research was hampered by the short observation time afforded by rockets. For long-term studies Giacconi encouraged construction of an Earth-orbiting X-ray satellite to survey the sky. Named Uhuru (launched 1970), it raised the number of known X-ray sources into the hundreds. Earlier, Giacconi had worked out the operating principles for a telescope that could focus X rays into images, and in the 1970s he built the first high-definition X-ray telescope. Called the Einstein Observatory (launched 1978), it examined stellar atmospheres and supernova remnants, identified many X-ray double stars (some containing suspected black holes), and detected X-ray sources in other galaxies. In 1976 Giacconi proposed a still more powerful instrument, which was finally launched in 1999 as the Chandra X-Ray Observatory.

## PRIZE ACCEPTANCE SPEECH

*Riccardo Giacconi's speech at the Nobel Banquet, December 10, 2002*

*Your Majesties, Your Royal Highnesses, Ladies and Gentlemen:*

A dinner speech is harder for me than a lecture. Therefore, I will simply share with you some of the feelings and thoughts I have had about this Nobel week.

At first, upon learning that we have become Nobel Laureates there is a feeling of personal pride which we share with family and friends. Then the realization hits us that the work for which we are honoured is the result of the cooperative effort of many many people over the years. Finally we feel a sense of continuity with the quest, initiated thousands of years ago for an understanding of the cosmos in which we live. While enormous strides have been made in the last decades, one of the most fundamental questions still have no answers, and so the quest goes on.

But other feelings and thoughts have come to the fore since reaching Stockholm. The warmth and kindness we have found here is expressed sometimes with solemnity and sometimes with whimsy and humor. We all feel we are participating in a great festival of lights. This week we are celebrating not only the light of reason, but also the light of poetry and art, the light of human solidarity and finally the lights of Santa Lucia.

It is a splendid reaffirmation of the human spirit and of our capacity to give meaning and warmth to life.

We are very grateful to you for the privilege of participating in these events. Thank you.

# ROY J. GLAUBER
## 2005

### INTRODUCTION

Roy Glauber was born in 1925 in New York City.

A member of the 1941 graduating class of the Bronx High School of Science, Glauber went on to do his undergraduate work at Harvard University.

After his sophomore year he was recruited to work on the Manhattan Project, where (at the age of 18) he was one of the youngest scientists at Los Alamos. His work involved calculating the critical mass for the atom bomb. After two years at Los Alamos, he returned to Harvard, receiving his bachelor's degree in 1946 and his PhD in 1949.

Glauber has received many honors for his research, including the A. A. Michelson Medal from the Franklin Institute in Philadelphia (1985), the Max Born Award from the Optical Society of America (1985), the Dannie Heineman Prize from the American Physical Society (1996), and the 2005 Nobel Prize in Physics.

He is currently the Mallinkrodt Professor of Physics at Harvard University, where both past and present students enthusiastically praised his teaching to Harvard Crimson reporters.

Glauber has two children, a son and a daughter, and five grandchildren.

Roy Glauber's recent research has dealt with problems in a number of areas of quantum optics, a field which, broadly speaking, studies the quantum electrodynamical interactions of light and matter. He is also continuing work on several topics in high- energy collision theory, including the analysis of hadron collisions, and the statistical correlation of particles produced in high-energy reactions.

Specific topics of his current research include: the quantum mechanical behavior of trapped wave packets; interactions of light with trapped ions; atom counting-the statistical properties of free atom beams and their measurement; algebraic methods for dealing with fermion statistics; coherence and correlations of bosonic atoms near the Bose-Einstein condensation; the theory of continuously monitored photon counting-and its reaction on quantum sources; the fundamental nature of "quantum jumps"; resonant transport of particles produced multiply in high-energy collisions; the multiple diffraction model of proton-proton and proton-antiproton scattering.

## PRIZE ACCEPTANCE SPEECH

*Roy J. Glauber's speech at the Nobel Banquet, December 10, 2005*

There are several equations left over from my talk on light last Thursday - and I thought this splendid dinner might be an ideal occasion to present them. But I'd like to say a few words first.

These dark days in Stockholm emphasize the importance of light in our lives. It is equally important in our literature. The word, "light", has vastly many meanings. Shakespeare, in *Love's Labours Lost*, has one of his cleverer characters make fun of that by speaking the line, "Light, seeking light, doth light of light beguile ..." Loosely translated, that means: Intellect, seeking understanding, easily fools reason. - Or perhaps it's the other way around.

Among these meanings for light you have lightness of weight or burden. In fact, when I read John Hall's and Ted Hänsch's huge lists of people they thanked for help in building lasers, I couldn't help recalling a Chinese proverb: "Many hands make light work." Our experimental friends must wonder in turn how theorists collaborate. How many theorists does it take, for example, to screw in a light bulb? The answer is three: One to climb the ladder and hold the bulb, a second to rotate the ladder, and a third to write about the rotation group and its double-valued representations.

There are many celebrations centered on the transcendent theme of light. I think of the Summer Solstice, in which I understand some picturesque northern folk spend Midsummer's Night dancing around Maypoles. But then there are also several celebrations, clustered around this darkest time of the year, that share the magical motif of light - the observance of the rebirth of the sun in many early cultures, the miracle of the oil lamps of the Maccabees, the Christians' new star shining in the East, and the candles of the martyred Santa Lucia,... But if this is the season to celebrate the rebirth of the sun, logic would tell you that Midsummer's Night must be the opposite. Still, you might have a hard time persuading the dancers on Midsummer's Night that they are celebrating a funeral. The sun, of course, doesn't have to die in order to be reborn every year. Now, that is also a metaphor for the way science progresses. Every field of study has its summer seasons, but must also be reborn from time to time.

We three physicists, a theorist and two experimental luminaries, are grateful to the Royal Academy and the Nobel Prize Committee for choosing this year to honor work on optics. Our work, we hope, is part of a rebirth of that science of light, and we are very pleased to see it rewarded in this most appropriate of seasons.

# ALBERT FERT
# 2007

## INTRODUCTION

Albert Fert (born March 7, 1938) is a French physicist and one of the discoverers of giant magnetoresistance which brought about a breakthrough in gigabyte hard disks. He is currently professor at Université Paris-Sud in Orsay and scientific director of a joint laboratory ('Unité mixte de recherche') between the Centre national de la recherche scientifique (National Scientific Research Centre) and Thales Group. He was awarded the 2007 Nobel Prize in Physics together with Peter Grünberg.

Fert graduated in 1962 from the École Normale Supérieure in Paris. He received his master's degree in 1963 at the University of Paris, and earned his PhD in 1970 at the Université Paris-Sud.

In 1988 Fert discovered the Giant magnetoresistance effect (GMR) in multilayers of iron and chromium which is recognized as the birth of spintronics; GMR was simultaneously and independently discovered by Peter Grünberg from the Jülich Research Centre. Since 1988, Albert Fert has made contributions to the field of spintronics.

1. American Physical Society International Prize for New Materials (1994)

2. Grand prix de physique

3. Jean Ricard of the French Physical Society (1994)

4.Centre National de la Recherche Scientifique Gold Medal

(2003)
5.Wolf Prize in Physics (2006)
6.Japan Prize (2007)
7. Nobel Prize in Physics (2007)

## PRIZE ACCEPTANCE SPEECH

*Albert Fert's speech at the Nobel Banquet, 10 December 2007*

Your Majesties, your Royal Highnesses, ladies and gentlemen, it is a great honour for Peter Grünberg and me to accept the Nobel Prize. We express our gratitude to the Royal Academy of Sciences and the Nobel Foundation. We want also to acknowledge the outstanding contributions to our work of many brilliant coworkers. I thank my coworkers, especially and directly those who are at this banquet today, I thank also my first guides in physics, my father, who was a physicist, a very acute physicist, Jacques Friedel and Ian Campbell, my guides at the time of my PhD, and, last but not least, I thank the partner for everything in my life, Marie-Josée, my wife.

I want also to tell you how another person, from Sweden, played certainly an important role for my orientation. When I was at he university, I liked physics, but I liked the arts too, I was a good photographer, I liked cinema, I wrote and I shot a film. My main inspiration was Ingmar Bergman, my god was Bergman. I remember trying to express the feelings I wanted to express by black and white close-up and slow panning shots, inspired by the first films of Bergman, Sommarlek, Sommaren med Monika, Smultronstället. But, when I saw my film, it was not at all expressing what I wanted to express, and I realized that, unfortunately, I was at light years from what I had seen in Bergman's films. But I could remember that I had some skills in physics, I began a PhD and I found that the research can be a very creative work too. The discovery of new and beautiful landscapes in the field of knowledge was also fascinating, and this led me to be here today, partly thanks to the inaccessibility of the genius of Ingmar Bergman.

On my way, I have discovered the beauty of sciences. It is amazing for a researcher to see the product of his ideas, of purely abstract constructions with electrons and spins, becoming a concrete reality of the everyday life. For Peter and me, it is amazing to realize that some of our ideas have led to applications we use everyday in our computer, something which is also useful to many people. Of course we have not been alone in this adventure. Spintronics has become a fruitful field of research thanks to the contributions of a very active international community and we are very pleased to acknowledge this collective contribution to the work which is recognized today.

# SERGE HAROCHE
# DAVID J. WINELAND
# 2012

## INTRODUCTION

**Serge Haroche** was born in 1944 in Casablanca. He graduated from Ecole Normale Supérieure (ENS), receiving his doctorate from Paris VI University in 1971 (thesis advisor: Claude Cohen-Tannoudji). After a post-doctoral visit to Stanford University in the laboratory of Arthur Schawlow (1972-73), he became full professor at Paris VI University in 1975, a position he held until 2001, when he was appointed Professor at Collège de France (Holder of the chair in quantum physics).

He has been Maitre de Conference at Ecole Polytechique (1974-1984), visiting professor at Harvard (1981), part time professor at Yale University (1984-1993), member of Institut Universitaire de France (1991-2000) and chairman of the ENS Department of Physics (1994-2000). His research has mostly taken place in laboratoire Kastler Brossel at ENS, where he now works with a team of senior coworkers, postdocs and graduate students.

Serge Haroche has received many prizes and awards, including the Grand Prix Jean Ricard of the French Physical Society (1983), the Einstein Prize for Laser science (1988), the Humbold Award (1992), the Michelson Medal from the Franklin Institute (1993), the Tomassoni Award from La Sapienza University (Rome, 2001), the Quantum Electronics prize of the European Physical Society (2002), the Quantum Communication Award of the International Organization for Quantum

Communication, Measurement and Computing (2002), the Townes Award of the Optical Society of America, the CNRS Gold Medal (2009), the Herbert Walter Prize of the German Physical Society and the Optical Society of America and the Nobel Prize in Physics, jointly awarded to David J. Wineland, (2012).

He is a member of the French Academy of Sciences and a Foreign Member of the National Academy of Sciences of the United States. He received in 2009 a five year advanced research grant from the European Research Council (ERC).

**David J. Wineland**, a physicist at the U.S. Department of Commerce's National Institute of Standards and Technology (NIST), has won the 2012 Nobel Prize in Physics. The honor is NIST's fourth Nobel prize in physics in the past 15 years.

Wineland shared the prize with Serge Haroche of the Collège de France and Ecole Normale Supérieure in Paris, France. In announcing the winners today, the Royal Swedish Academy of Sciences cited Wineland and Haroche "for ground-breaking experimental methods that enable measuring and manipulation of individual quantum systems."

## PRIZE ACCEPTANCE SPEECH

*Serge Haroche delivering his banquet speech.*

*Your Majesties, your Royal Highnesses, Dear Friends and Colleagues, Ladies and Gentlemen,*

Let me, at the close of this wonderful banquet, evoke the memory of Erwin Schrödinger. His work has had an impact on all the fields of science and culture celebrated tonight. He received the Nobel prize in Physics in 1933 for finding the equation which explains the behavior of matter at the quantum level. Schrödinger's equation also accounts, at least in principle, for the structure of all the molecules studied in chemistry and biology. It has also a strong influence on the world economy. Most of the devices which have changed our lives are based on quantum physics, from the laser to the transistor, from the GPS to the cell phone, from the magnetic resonance imaging to the global communication network. Schrödinger's equation is essential to explain the workings of these technological marvels, whose sales reach billions of dollars.

What about Schrödinger's merits in literature? He may not have written any novel, but he invented a character about which a lot has been written in many books, a character which has even featured in movies, generating endless metaphysical discussions. I am of course referring to the legendary Schrödinger's cat, suspended between life and death by the laws of quantum physics and its superposition principle. In his famous thought experiment, Schrödinger could have chosen an inanimate object or a less lovable living being, a cockroach for instance. Just think about it. What about Schrödinger's cockroach? The story would have been as demonstrative to explain the strange logic of the quantum world, but much less impressive. By the stroke of genius of choosing the right animal in the right dramatic situation, and by having fathered an immortal character as famous as the Cheshire cat of Alice in Wonderland, Schrödinger has made an impact on the world culture.

My fondness for this quantum feline is of course biased. David Wineland and I have been awarded the Nobel Prize for creating miniature versions of this famous cat, made of a few atoms or photons. We have both been accompanied in our long research adventure by wonderful colleagues, without whom we would never have succeeded. We are very glad that many of them are here this evening. Other groups in the world are also working in this field, raising various ersatz of laboratory cats and trying to preserve as long as possible their quantumness. What is the future of these cats? One easy - may be too easy - answer, is that they will turn into a quantum computer. I don't know. I rather guess that they will lead to some unforeseen application, even more astonishing than this mythical machine. When the minister Gladstone asked Faraday what his research on electricity could be good for, the nineteen century physicist replied "One day, sir, you may tax it". We are tempted to give our politicians the same answer: "One day, you may tax Schrödinger's cat".

I must add though that, if someone was dubious about the taxability of his cat, it was Schrödinger. Not believing that it would one day be possible to really perform such experiments, he once wrote: "We never experiment with just one electron, or atom or small molecule. In thought experiments, we assume that we do; this invariably entails ridiculous consequences". In spite of the admiration we have for Schrödinger, my friend David Wineland and I must on this point disagree with him: for us, the consequences, culminating in this magnificent evening, have been far from ridiculous!

# MEDICINE

## RONALD ROSS
## 1902

### INTRODUCTION

RONALD ROSS was born on May 13, 1857, as the son of Sir C.C.G. Ross, a General in the English army. He commenced the study of medicine at St. Bartholomew's Hospital in London in 1875; entered the Indian Medical Service in 1881. He commenced the study of malaria in 1892. In 1894 he determined to make an experimental investiga-tion in India of the hypothesis of Laveran and Manson that mosquitoes are connected with the propagation of the disease. After two and a half years' failure, Ross succeeded in demonstrating the life-cycle of the parasites of malaria in mosquitoes, thus establishing the hypothesis of Laveran and Manson. In 1899 he joined the Liverpool School of Tropical Medicine under the direction of Sir Alfred Jones. He was immediately sent to West Africa to continue his investigations, and there he found the species of mosquitoes which convey the deadly African fever. Since then the School has been unremitting in its efforts to improve health, and especially to reduce the malaria in West Africa. Ross' researches have been confirmed and assisted by many distinguished authorities, especially by Koch, Daniels, Bignami, Celli, Christophers, Stephens, Annett, Austen, Ruge, Ziemann, and many others.

In 1901 Ross was elected a Fellow of the Royal College of Surgeons of England and also a Fellow of the Royal Society, of which he became Vice-President from 1911 to 1913. In 1902 he was appointed a Companion of the Most Honourable Order of Bath by His Majesty the King of Great Britain. In 1911 he was elevated to the rank of Knight Commander of the same Order. In Belgium, he was made an Officer in the Order of Leopold II.

In 1926 he assumed the post of Director in Chief of the Ross Institute and Hospital of Tropical Diseases and Hygiene, which had been created by admirers of his work, and he remained in this position until his death. He was also a President of the Society of Tropical Medicine.

He made many contributions to the epidemiology of malaria and to methods of its survey and assessment, but perhaps his greatest was the development of mathematical models for the study of its epidemiology, initiated in his report on Mauritius in 1908, elaborated in his *Prevention of Malaria* in 1911 and further elaborated in a more generalized form in scientific papers published by the Royal Society in 1915 and 1916.

He received many honours in addition to the Nobel Prize, and was given Honorary Membership of learned societies of most countries of Europe, and of many other continents. He got an honorary M.D. degree in Stockholm in 1910 at the centenary celebration of the Caroline Institute.

Ross married Rosa Bessie Bloxam in 1889. They had two sons, Ronald and Charles, and two daughters, Dorothy and Sylvia. His wife died in 1931, Ross survived her until a year later, when he died after a long illness, at the Ross Institute, London, on September 16, 1932.

## PRIZE ACCEPTANCE SPEECH

*Ronald Ross's speech at the Nobel Banquet in Stockholm, December 10, 1902*

*Your Royal Highnesses, grefve Mörner and gentlemen,*

I beg to thank you for the very great honour you have done me in drinking to my health this evening; and you, Professor Mörner, for the eloquent and flattering terms in which you proposed the toast. I beg to accept the honour, not only for myself, but for all those who have laboured so long at the important subject of malaria. Permit me, at this auspicious moment, to mention the names of some of those to whom humanity owes so much, but who have not always been as fortunate as myself in receiving reward for their labours. I will begin with the great name of Laveran, who more than twenty years ago discovered the cause of malaria and created a new branch of science - Laveran, that true man of science who has honoured me by permitting me to call him my master. I will mention next the names of Golgi, that most distinguished Italian; of Danilewsky, of Marchiafava, and Celli, of Kelsch, of Mannaberg, of Bignami, Romanowsky, Sakharof, Canalis, Bastianelli, Dionisi, Vandyke Carter, the two Plehns, Ziemann, Thayer, and not least, MacCallum, who, with a host of others no less meritorious, consolidated the discovery of Laveran. Turning now to the subject of malaria and mosquitoes, I must first mention those who created the hypothesis, namely King, in America, Koch, in Germany, Laveran, in France, and particularly Manson, in England, whose profound induction formed the basis of my own humble endeavours, and whom I shall always esteem one of my masters. Now permit me the honour of naming those who in all parts of the world confirmed and amplified those elements of the truth which I had found in India - the great Koch and his German colleagues; Bignami, Bastianelli, and Celli, in Italy; Daniels, Stephens, Christophers, Ziemann, Annett, Dutton, Elliott, Van der Scheer, Van Birlekom, Manson and his son, Fernside James, Nuttall, Austen, Theobald, Howard and many others. Nor let us by any means forget those who are endeavouring to turn these discoveries to practical account for the saving of human life on a large scale, particularly Koch, Sir William MacGregor, Celli, Logan Taylor and Gorgas; and, not least, Sir Alfred Jones and those merchants of London and Liverpool who are spending their money freely for the same great cause.

In conclusion, gentlemen, I hope you will permit me to utter a personal note. I cannot help comparing the present moment with that when, seven years ago, I commenced the researches for which you have today given me such great honour. I cannot help remembering the dingy little military hospital, the old cracked microscope, and the medicine bottles which constituted all the laboratory and apparatus which I possessed for the purpose of attacking one of the most redoubtable of scientific problems. Today I have received in this most beautiful capital of the north, the most distinguished of all scientific honours from the hand of your king himself. Gentlemen, I can do no more than thank you.

# ARCHIBALD V. HILL
## 1922

### INTRODUCTION

ARCHIBALD VIVIAN HILL was born in Bristol on September 26,1886. His early education was at Blundell's School, Tiverton, whence he obtained scholarships to Trinity College, Cambridge. Here he studied mathematics and took the Mathematical Tripos, being Third Wrangler (1907). After graduating, he was urged to take up physiology by his teacher, Dr. (later Sir) Walter Morley Fletcher.

Hill started his research work in 1909. It was due to J.N. Langley, Head of the Department of Physiology at that time that Hill took up the study on the nature of muscular contraction.

After having obtained a Fellowship at Trinity in 1910, Hill spent the winter of 1910-1911 in Germany, working among others with Bürker (who taught him much about the technique of myothermic observations) and Paschen (who introduced the galvanometer to him, which he since used for his investigations). From 1911-1914, until the outbreak of World War I, he continued his work on the physiology of muscular contraction at Cambridge.

In 1914 he tended to drift away from physiology and was actually appointed University Lecturer in Physical Chemistry at Cambridge.

In 1919 he took up again his study of the physiology of muscle, and came into close contact with Meyerhof of Kiel who, approaching the problem from a different angle, has arrived at results closely analogous to his study.

In 1920 Hill was appointed Brackenburg Professor of Physiology at Manchester University; there he continued the work on muscular activity and began to apply the results obtained on isolated muscles to the case of muscular exercise in man. From 1923 to 1925 he became Jodrell Professor of Physiology at University College, London, succeeding E.H. Starling. In 1926 he was appointed the Royal Society's Foulerton Research Professor and was in charge of the Biophysics Laboratory at University College until 1952.

Dr. Hill is the author of many scientific papers, lectures, and books. Perhaps his best-known books are *Muscular Activity* (1926), *Muscular Movement in Man* (1927); also *Living Machinery* (1927), *The Ethical Dilemma of Science and Other Writings* (1960), and *Traits and Trials in Physiotogy* (1965).

He is also a member of the Society for the Protection of Science and Learning, and was President in 1952 of the British Society for the Advancement of Science.

Dr. Hill married Margaret Neville Keynes in 1913. Archibald V. Hill died on June 3, 1977.

## PRIZE ACCEPTANCE SPEECH

*Archibald V. Hill's speech at the Nobel Banquet in Stockholm, December 10, 1923*

The pursuit of natural knowledge, the investigation of the world - mental and material - in which we live, is not a dull and spiritless affair: rather is it a voyage of adventure of the human mind, a holiday for reckless and imaginative souls. It is natural, therefore, that a people such as yours, descended from soldiers and adventurers, should wish to rejoice with those who return from the deep waters and the distant lands of discovery. I reflected, however, on first thoughts, that you go too far, you are too generous, in your rejoicing with them. Those whose lives are so filled with the romance of discovery, whose years are a holiday of exploration, do not need, do not deserve, payment for their toil. Their work itself is adequate reward, they have more happiness already than their share; and here you come - undemocratically in a democratic world - exaggerating the unevenness of its distribution. Many luckless people imagine that romance is dead: some, overcivilised, fondly suppose that there never was romance: a poet tells us that romance is unrecognised though really present: but scientists can meet him daily, walking at large and undisguised in the world. Perhaps therefore - on second thoughts - you are right, in aiding those who wish to devote themselves to discovery, in rewarding those who assure the world of the reality of romance. Perhaps the spirit of adventure, be it mental or material adventure, is a factor so essential in human progress, that no emphasis of it is undue. It is not for us at any rate, the recipients of your generosity, to quarrel with your decision: indeed no satisfaction could be greater than that afforded by the gift and the honour which you, and your country, have lavished upon us.

As the spiritual disciple of your great physiologist Blix, of Lund, I recognise that there are other essentials factors in scientific progress: namely cooperation between men and brotherhood between nations. But for an international meeting where Professor Langley of Cambridge obtained a certain delicate instrument from Prof. Blix of Lund, I should not be here today. Kindliness and sympathy, fellowship and understanding, are always good, but best when they come from a distant corner of the world. There is something complete and universal about an international kindness, an international compliment, a Nobel Prize: they bring men together, they take no account of race or creed: the old and the young, the little and great are alike, so that knowledge be promoted. The War tore asunder two parts of the world as essential to one another as man and wife. Physiology, I am glad to know, was the first science to forget the hatreds and follies of the War and to revive a truly international Congress: my own country, I am proud to boast, was happy to be its meeting-ground. For a while, my friend Meyerhof was an enemy: today he is again a colleague and a friend. Only three months ago, little suspecting the occasion of our next meeting, we were walking for several days together in the Donauthal, after another Congress, discussing occasionally the neutralisation of the Rhine, but generally the neutralisation of acid in frog's muscle. We are glad to feel that your joint award to us, however unworthy we may know ourselves to be, is a seal of your approval, the approval of a people friendly to my nation and to his nation, of a brotherhood in Science between a German and an Englishman.

Two things, therefore, are emphasised by our presence here today, the romance and adventure of discovery, and the brotherhood of Science. I may be unworthy of your praise: I am not ungrateful for your generosity: and from my heart I thank you, not only for the honour and happiness you have given me, but for your emphasis of these two essential human factors in the progress of human knowledge.

# SIR FREDERICK HOPKINS
# 1929

## INTRODUCTION

FREDERICK GOWLAND HOPKINS was born on June 20, 1861, at Eastbourne, England. His father, a bookseller in Bishopsgate Street, London, was much interested in science, but he died when Gowland was an infant. For the next ten years Gowland lived with his mother at Eastbourne, showing as a child literary rather than scientific tastes, although, when his mother gave him a microscope, he studied life on the seashore.

In 1871 his mother went to live at Enfield, and Hopkins went to the city of London School. He was a bright schoolboy in several subjects, and was given a first-class in chemistry in 1874. Later, as a result of an examination at the College of Preceptors he was given a prize for science, and, at the early age of 17, when he finally left school, he published a paper in *The Entomologist* on the bombardier beetle.

He was then 22 years old, and he took part in several important legal cases. He then decided to take his London B.Sc. degree and graduated in the shortest possible time. In 1888, when he was 28, he went as a medical student to Guy's Hospital, London, and was immediately given the Sir William Gull Studentship there. He was awarded, during this period, a Gold Medal for Chemistry, and Honours in Materia Medica.

In 1894, when he was 32 years old, he graduated in medicine and taught for four years physiology and toxicology at Guy's Hospital. For two years he was in charge of the Chemical Department of the Clinical Research Association. In 1896 he published, with H.W. Brook, work on the halogen derivatives of proteins, and in 1898, work with S. N. Pinkus on the crystallization of blood albumins. In 1898, when attending a meeting of the Physiological Society at Cambridge, he was invited by Sir Michael Foster to move to Cambridge to develop there the chemical aspects of physiology.

In 1902 he was given a readership in biochemistry, and in 1910 he became a Fellow of Trinity College, and an Honorary Fellow of Emmanuel College. In 1914 he was elected to the Chair of Biochemistry at Cambridge University.

Subsequently he did the work which was to gain him in 1929, together with Christiaan Eijkman, who had demonstrated the association between beriberi and the consumption of decorticated rice, the Nobel Prize. Later, Hopkins worked with Walter Fletcher on the metabolic changes occurring in muscular contractions and rigor mortis. Hopkins supplied exact methods of analysis, and devised a new colour reaction for lactic acid, and the pioneer work then done laid the foundations for the work of the Nobel Laureates, A.V. Hill and Otto Meyerhof, and also for that of many other later workers.

In 1898 Hopkins married Jessie Anne Stevens. They had two daughters, one of whom Jacquetta Hawkes, is married to J. B. Priestley, the author.

Hopkins died in 1947, at the age of 86.

## PRIZE ACCEPTANCE SPEECH

*Sir Frederick Hopkins's speech at the Nobel Banquet in Stockholm, December 10, 1929*

Your Royal Highnesses, Your Excellencies, Ladies and Gentlemen, Nobel Laureates are greatly privileged. Their privileges, I venture to say, begin with the invitation to Stockholm, and with the circumstances which meet them there. Stockholm takes care that a fitting stage is provided for the conferment of honours which carry such lasting prestige.

A student of civilisation who visits this City for the first time realises that his education had till then been incomplete. It is not alone the great beauty of her situation, - nor even this combined with the thrilling successes of her modern architects and her to-day's intensive enterprises, - which causes Stockholm to make so unique an impression. It is something that has yet deeper foundations. If I may give humble expression to a personal feeling, I would say that it is because, more than other Capitals, Stockholm expresses the genius of a race; the very spirit of the great northern race which has slowly created her.

For the Nobel Prize-winner the privileges of a visit to Stockholm receive a manifold increase. He ceases, indeed, for the time, to feel mortal! Surely nowhere, and at no time, have honours been conferred upon individuals with greater generosity of effort, or with ceremonies more full of artistic fitness, than Stockholm provides for these occasions. The treatment enjoyed by Laureates would surely have given pleasure to him whose testament was the origin of all such efforts, to him who was a man of imagination as well as a man of affairs.

Even Stockholm with all her distinctions must feel that she gains prestige from the circumstance that within her boundaries is administered, with meticulous care and with a justice which transcends all narrow national considerations, so great a trust as that created by the testament of Alfred Nobel. The administration of that Trust does more than reward individual efforts. Its magnificently generous policy stirs the imagination of all countries. Year by year it reminds a world too prone to be indifferent to such matters that the advance of knowledge, the glory of literature, and the advent of peace must depend upon individual efforts, and that rewards may be due, and are to be won, which are not those of the marketplace or the political arena.

In acknowledging my own great good fortune as a chosen Laureate I cannot refrain from referring to the circumstance that the subject I profess, the comparatively young science of Biochemistry, has this year, in effect if not by name, received no less than four Nobel prizes. Those allotted to Medicine, and no less those to Chemistry, have been awarded for researches all of which were essentially contributions to Biochemistry!

I have called it a young science; but it is after all not so young, though its phase of vigorous progress is recent. A century ago Stockholm was already seeing the beginnings of modern Biochemistry. A hundred years ago Berzelius, having attained to leisure by resigning - I think - his chief duties at the Caroline Institute (I must be careful in my statements since Professor Söderbaum is present), was seeing through the Press the proofs of his "Thierchemie".

Indeed, exactly one hundred years ago to the very day, Wöhler, who, as you know, had been Berzelius's devoted pupil and assistant, wrote from Berlin to the great Swede in Stockholm a letter dated December 10th 1829 in which he acknowledges the receipt of proofs of part of the "Thierchemie". To say the truth, Wöhler proceeds in this letter to sympathise with its author for having to deal with such a tangle of chemistry, anatomy, physiology and unproven data as the subject then comprised. One would like to know how Wöhler would appraise the subject to-day; and I wonder (as many must have wondered) what would have been the emotions of Berzelius could he have foreseen all the benefits that chemical science was to receive in these later days from the city of his own activities.

I have spoken as a biochemist, but I must remember that in the regretted absence of Professor Eijkman I am the sole representative of the Laureates for Medicine. The progress of Biochemistry, it must be admitted, has become one of the chief contributions to the progress of modern Medicine. Speaking for the moment on behalf of the latter, I should like to bear witness to the wide recognition in England of our debt to Sweden. It is recognised, to take but one instance, that in the technique of the curative use of radium Stockholm has led the world and taught lessons to all. When, this afternoon, I received from His Majesty the tokens of Laureateship, I realised afresh how little I had expected the honour, and I was led to ask myself, not for the first time, the perhaps debatable question: Are honours and rewards the more desirable in the days of full vigour or after most of one's work is done? I am not sure that the more obvious answer is the right one. Youth, it is true, needs sustenance, but should need no tonic. The pulse of age may be quickened by the recognition of past efforts and unsuspected capacity for further effort thus revealed. I myself, at any rate, rejoice in the moment of my good fortune. The great gift from Sweden awakens my deepest gratitude.

# SIR CHARLES SHERRINGTON
# 1932

## INTRODUCTION

CHARLES SCOTT SHERRINGTON was born on November 27, 1857, at Islington, London. He was the son of James Norton Sherrington, of Caister, Great Yarmouth, who died when Sherrington was a young child. Sherrington's mother later married Dr. Caleb Rose of Ipswich, a good classical scholar and a noted archaeologist, whose interest in the English artists of the Norwich School no doubt gave Sherrington the interest in art that he retained throughout his life.

In 1876 Sherrington began medical studies at St. Thomas's Hospital and in 1878 passed the primary examination of the Royal College of Surgeons, and a year later the primary examination for the Fellowship of that College. After a short stay at Edinburgh he went, in 1879, to Cambridge as a noncollegiate student studying physiology under Michael Foster, and in 1880 entered Gonville and Caius College there.

In 1881 he attended a medical congress in London at which Sir Michael Foster discussed the work of Sir Charles Bell and others on the experimental study of the functions of nerves that was then being done in England and elsewhere in Europe.

In 1883 Sherrington became Demonstrator of Anatomy at Cambridge under Professor Sir George Humphrey, and during the winter session of 1883-1884 at St. Thomas's Hospital he demonstrated histology.

The years 1884 and 1885 were eventful ones for Sherrington,

for during the winter of 1884-1885 he worked with Goltz at Strasbourg, in 1884 he obtained his M.R.C.S., and in 1885 a First Class in the Natural Sciences Tripos at Cambridge with distinction.

In 1906 he published his well-known book: *The Integrative Action of the Nervous System*, being his Silliman Lectures held at Yale University the previous year, and in 1913 he was invited to become Waynfleet Professor of Physiology at Oxford, a post for which he had unsuccessfully applied in 1895, and here he remained until his retirement in 1936. Here he wrote, and published in 1919, his classic book entitled *Mammalian Physiology: a Course of Practical Exercises*, and here he regularly taught the students for whom this book was written.

Sherrington was elected a Fellow of the Royal Society of London in 1893, where he gave the Croonian Lecture in 1897, and was awarded the Royal Medal in 1905 and the Copley Medal in 1927. In 1922 the Knight Grand Cross of the Order of the British Empire and in 1924 the Order of Merit were conferred upon him. He held honorary doctorates of the Universities of Oxford, London, Sheffield, Birmingham, Manchester, Liverpool, Wales, Edinburgh, Glasgow, Paris, Strasbourg, Louvain, Uppsala, Lyons, Budapest, Athens, Brussels, Berne, Toronto, Montreal, and Harvard.

In 1892 Sherrington married Ethel Mary, daughter of John Ely Wright, of Preston Manor, Suffolk. After some years of frail health, during which, however, he remained mentally very alert, he died suddenly of heart failure at Eastbourne in 1952.

*Sir Charles Sherrington died on March 4, 1952.*

## PRIZE ACCEPTANCE SPEECH

*Sir Charles Sherrington's speech at the Nobel Banquet in Stockholm, December 10, 1932*

*Your Royal Highnesses, Your Excellencies, Ladies and Gentlemen.*

I rise in response to the kind toast given by Professor Gunnar Holmgren, and I esteem it a privilege to tender my thanks to him, in this company and in this City renowned for its hospitality, for the generous words which have been spoken. The compliment of the award of a Nobel Prize I value the more since I can interpret it as a sign of sympathetic interest in the efforts of experimental neurology, no less than a generous encouragement to myself.

Several circumstances enhance for me the enjoyment of this visit to Sweden. In the first place it is a pleasure to meet here Swedish scientific men whose names are known the world over, and among them some whom I have known long enough to venture to call them old friends. Then, for one whose study concerns nerves and their activity, it is since nerves express themselves through muscular action, of special interest to visit Sweden with its high tradition of masters in the science of muscular action, for instance Magnus Blix, and Professor Johansson. Further, it is delightful to be associated in this visit with my friend, Professor Adrian, who treats the nerves as a sort of electric power house, and makes even their minutest leakages audible to us. With him we can, so to say, hear the gold fish 'thinking', a new fairy-tale for Christmas Eve, now nearly here.

May I take this opportunity to pay a word of tribute on general lines to the work of the Nobel Foundation for the welfare of Science. It must be a difficult thing to adjudicate prizes where so much research and discovery are going on and where so many researchers are deserving. I am sure I am voicing a universal opinion when I say that the considerate care and sympathetic width of view which the Foundation has consistently shown has enhanced the prestige of the Prizes themselves in the eyes of the cultivated world. Its doing so has been a source of deep satisfaction and encouragement to Science itself.

May I remark that a happy and inspiring note in this annual celebration which must have impressed us all in the Concert Hall today is the dignity and charm of the ceremonial observed. Such observance proclaims that Science is worthy of an aesthetic as well as of a purely intellectual setting; and that emphasis is of itself a service to Science.

When we think of Alfred Nobel we cannot but remember that along with his devotion to Science, he was an idealist with lofty ideals. He was, for the thing, an ardent advocate of international friendship and of cooperation between nations. He saw as every thinking man must see, an illustration of the possibilities of that cooperation in the collaboration of scientific researchers the civilized world over in the advance of Science. Nothing can have exemplified better the solidarity of the civilized world in the pursuit of Science than the record of the awards of the Nobel Foundation since their inception a quarter of a century ago. That record instances now this country, now that, often two different countries together, according as the international stream of progress winds. It is the progress of the stream which matters. That holds an added pleasure for each recipient - because each can then feel that his recognition has come to him not in virtue of anything he has done for himself in the sense of for his own sake but because he has contributed a piece - in my case I feel it is a very humble piece - to the advancement of a great common cause. I thank you.

# EDGAR ADRIAN
## 1932

### INTRODUCTION

EDGAR DOUGLAS ADRIAN was born on November 30, 1889, in London. He was the second son of Alfred Douglas Adrian, C.B., K.C., legal adviser to the British Local Government Board. Adrian went to school at Westminster School, London, and in 1908 he went to Trinity College, Cambridge, at which College he had won a Scholarship in Science. At Cambridge University he studied physiology and the other subjects of the Natural Sciences Tripos and in 1911 he took his B.A. degree with first classes in five separate subjects.

In 1913 he was elected to a Fellowship of Trinity College on account of his investigation of the «all or none» principle in nerve. He then studied medicine, doing his clinical work at St. Bartholomew's Hospital, London, and taking his medical degree in 1915. In 1925 he began investigating the sense organs by electrical methods.

In 1929 he was elected Foulerton Professor of the Royal Society. In 1937 he succeeded Sir Joseph Barcroft as Professor of Physiology at the University of Cambridge, a post which he held until 1951.

In 1951 Adrian was elected Master of Trinity College, Cambridge, a post which he still, at the time of writing, holds.

Subsequently, Adrian studied the sense of smell and the electrical activity of the brain and the variations and abnormalities of waves shown in the encephalogram, which

Hans Berger, of Jena, had described in 1929. This work opened up new fields of investigation in the study of epilepsy and other lesions of the brain. For his work about the functions of neurones Adrian was awarded, jointly with Sir Charles Sherrington, the Nobel Prize for 1932.

The results of Adrian's brilliant researches on the electrophysiology of the brain and nervous system were published in numerous scientific papers and in his three books, *The Basis of Sensation* (1927), *The Mechanism of Nervous Action* (1932) and *The Physical Basis of Perception* (1947). With others he wrote *Factors Determining Human Behaviour* (1937).

Adrian had numerous honours bestowed upon him. During 1950-1955 he was President of the Royal Society, and during 1960-1962 of the Royal Society of Medicine. In 1954, he was President of the British Association for the Advancement of Science. He is Chevalier of the French Legion of Honour and a trustee of the Rockefeller Institute. He holds honorary degrees, memberships, and fellowships of numerous universities and other learned bodies. He was knighted Baron of Cambridge in 1955.

In 1923 Adrian married Hester Agnes Pinsent, daughter of the late Hume Pinsent of Birmingham, England, and a relative of the philosoper David Hume. They have one son and two daughters. *Edgar Adrian died on August 8, 1977.*

## PRIZE ACCEPTANCE SPEECH

*Edgar Adrian's speech at the Nobel Banquet in Stockholm, December 10, 1932*

*Your Royal Highness, your Excellencies, my Lords, Ladies and Gentlemen*

In my College at Cambridge - Trinity College - all of us know of Stockholm as the beautiful capital of a country which has a great history and is now in the forefront of modern civilisation. There are some of us who try very hard to copy your artistic enterprise and to decorate our houses in the Swedish manner, and our learned societies can be divided into two classes - those who have attended an international congress at Stockholm and those who have not, and do not know, therefore, how pleasant such events can be.

Trinity is a very large College, but however large we were

we should still be immensely proud of the fact that in the past no less than eight of us have had a special reason to praise your hospitality. Eight of the Fellows of Trinity have had reason to look back on their visit here as an outstanding event in their lives, for eight have made the winter journey to attend the Nobel celebrations and have gone back far the richer - richer in pocket of course - but richer too in the tremendous encouragement which comes from such an award.

Eight Nobel prizemen is a large number, and however great your admiration for science you may wonder whether one cannot have too much of a good thing! You may fancy that a College in which eight Nobel prizemen live together would not be a very comfortable place for anybody else. But I have really exaggerated our good fortune for in fact only two of our prizemen live in the College and only four in Cambridge.

And now I make the ninth to come on the same errand and even after today's impressive ceremony I still find it very hard to believe that so high an honour should have fallen to me. But at least I have had one special advantage among scientific workers. For five years I lived in Cambridge in the rooms which belonged, nearly 300 years ago, to the great astronomer and physicist, Sir Isaac Newton. He had a living room and a study looking out on to the Great Court of Trinity and a small and very cold bedroom.

Newton was our greatest English scientist and I do not think that anyone living in such surroundings could fail to be infected with the spirit of scientific enquiry. Perhaps in these days we do not regard the laws of gravitation with the same reverence as did our fathers, but we have, unfortunately, more reason to be impressed by his ability in another field - for much of his life was spent in London in the Government Service reorganising the coinage of England in a way which did much to restore prosperity at a time when it was badly needed.

But although I have lived in such inspiring surroundings, in another way I suffer from my upbringing. As you know from Mr Galsworthy's novels, in my country we are not skilled at expressing our emotions and we are not encouraged to do so, whatever we may feel. And so now I feel very great happiness and very deep gratitude to the memory of Alfred Nobel, to the Committee and to you all, but all that I can find to say is "Thank you very much indeed!"

# SIR ALEXANDER FLEMING
## 1945

### INTRODUCTION

SIR ALEXANDER FLEMING was born at Lochfield near Darvel in Ayrshire, Scotland on August 6th, 1881. He attended Louden Moor School, Darvel School, and Kilmarnock Academy before moving to London where he attended the Polytechnic. He spent four years in a shipping office before entering St. Mary's Medical School, London University. He qualified with distinction in 1906 and began research at St. Mary's under Sir Almroth Wright, a pioneer in vaccine therapy. He gained M.B., B.S., (London), with Gold Medal in 1908, and became a lecturer at St. Mary's until 1914. He served throughout World War I as a captain in the Army Medical Corps, being mentioned in dispatches, and in 1918 he returned to St.Mary's. He was elected Professor of the School in 1928 and Emeritus Professor of Bacteriology, University of London in 1948. He was elected Fellow of the Royal Society in 1943 and knighted in 1944.

Fleming, a Fellow of the Royal College of Surgeons (England), 1909, and a Fellow of the Royal College of Physicians (London), 1944, has gained many awards. They include Hunterian Professor (1919), Arris and Gale Lecturer (1929) and Honorary Gold Medal (1946) of the Royal College of Surgeons; Williams Julius Mickle Fellowship, University of London (1942); Charles Mickle Fellowship, University of Toronto (1944); John Scott Medal, City Guild of Philadelphia (1944); Cameron Prize, University of Edinburgh (1945); Moxon Medal, Royal College of

Physicians (1945); Cutter Lecturer, Harvard University (1945); Albert Gold Medal, Royal Society of Arts (1946); Gold Medal, Royal Society of Medicine (1947); Medal for Merit, U.S.A. (1947); and the Grand Cross of Alphonse X the Wise, Spain (1948).

He served as President of the Society for General Microbiology, he was a Member of the Pontifical Academy of Science and Honorary Member of almost all the .medical and scientific societies of the world. He was Rector of Edinburgh University during 1951-1954, Freeman of many boroughs and cities and Honorary Chief Doy-gei-tau of the Kiowa tribe. He was also awarded doctorate, *honoris causa,* degrees of almost thirty European and American Universities.

In 1915, Fleming married Sarah Marion McElroy of Killala, Ireland, who died in 1949. Their son is a general medical practitioner.

Fleming married again in 1953, his bride was Dr. Amalia Koutsouri-Voureka, a Greek colleague at St. Mary's. Dr Fleming died on March 11th in 1955 and is buried in St. Paul's Cathedral.

## PRIZE ACCEPTANCE SPEECH

*Sir Alexander Fleming's speech at the Nobel Banquet in Stockholm, December 10, 1945*

For many years I have read of people getting the Nobel Prize. Then I always regarded them as a superior class to which it was almost impossible to aspire. Now suddenly I find myself in that class and I wonder whether they are so different.

Did they obtain this great distinction - for indeed it is the greatest distinction a scientist can obtain - by deep thought or did Dame Fortune play a part.

We all know that chance, fortune, fate or destiny - call it what you will has played a considerable part in many of the great discoveries in science. We do not know how many, for all scientists who have hit on something new have not disclosed exactly how it happened. We do know, though, that in many cases it was a chance observation which took them into a track which eventually led to a real advance in knowledge or practice. This is especially true of the biological sciences for there we are dealing with living mechanisms about which there are enormous gaps in our knowledge.

I am here because of penicillin and perhaps the story of penicillin illustrates what I am saying.

I myself have since the introduction of Salvarsan 35 years ago been interested in chemotherapy and antiseptics. But I was really an immunologist, working in a laboratory almost entirely devoted to immunology. In 1922 by a combination of fortuitous circumstances I discovered lysozyme - one of the most interesting antibiotic substances. The extraordinary bacteriolytic power of lysozyme - a ferment present in our normal cells and secretions - especially in such supposedly inert secretion as the tears - showed me how powerful an antibiotic substance could be. Unfortunately lysozyme acted most strongly on the wrong microbes (from the medical point of view) - those which did not infect man - but it had its uses for it paved the way for penicillin for me and I think also for my partners in this Nobel Award, Sir Howard Florey and Dr. Chain.

Then in 1928 an accidental contamination of a culture plate by a mould set me off on another track. I was working on a subject having no relation to moulds or antiseptics and if I had been a member of a team engaged on this subject it is likely that I would have had to neglect the accidental happening and work for the team with the result that penicillin would not then have been described and I would not be here today as a Nobel Laureate. But, fortunately for myself - and may be for the world - I was situated so that I could leave my previous line of research work and follow the track which fate hade indicated for me.

I isolated the contaminating mould. It made an antibacterial substance which I christened penicillin. I studied it as far as I could as a bacteriologist. I had a clue that here was something good but I could not possibly know how good it was and I had not the team, especially the chemical team, necessary to concentrate and stabilise the penicillin.

It was ten years later that Florey and Chain made up a complete team at Oxford which succeeded in this and showed the marvellous chemotherapeutic properties of penicillin.

Then fortune again intervened for they obtained their results in the midst of a great war when ordinary economics are in abeyance and large scale production could go ahead as it would never have done in times of peace. The result is that in an incredibly short time manufacturing difficulties have been overcome and penicillin is being produced on a large scale.

I have been trying to use penicillin to illustrate two points.

The first is that team work may inhibit the primary initiation of something quite new but once a clue has been obtained team work may be absolutely necessary to bring the discovery to full advantage.

The second is that destiny may play a large part in discovery. It was destiny which contaminated my culture plate in 1928 - it was destiny which led Chain and Florey in 1938 to investigate penicillin instead of the many other antibiotics which had then been described and it was destiny that timed their work to come to fruition in war-time when penicillin was most needed.

It may be that while we think we are masters of the situation we are merely pawns being moved about on the board of life by some superior power.

Thank you.

# EDWARD C. KENDALL
# 1950

## INTRODUCTION

EDWARD CALVIN KENDALL was born on March 8, 1886, at South Norwalk, Connecticut, U.S.A. He was educated at Columbia University, where he obtained the degrees of Bachelor of Science in 1908 and Master of Science, specializing in Chemistry, in 1909. From 1909 until 1910 he was Goldschmidt Fellow of this University, and in 1910 he obtained his Ph.D. in Chemistry.

From 1910 until 1911 he was research chemist for Parke, Davis and Co., at Detroit, Michigan, U.S.A. Here he did research on the thyroid gland, and from 1911 until 1914 he continued this work at St. Luke's Hospital, New York.

In 1914 he was appointed Head of the Biochemistry Section in the Graduate School of the Mayo Foundation, Rochester which is part of the University of Minnesota, and in 1915 he was appointed Director of the Division of Biochemistry there and subsequently Professor of Physiological Chemistry. On April 1, 1951, Kendall reached the age of retirement from the Mayo Foundation and he accepted the position of Visiting Professor in the Department of Biochemistry at Princeton University, a position, which at the time of writing, he still holds.

After many years the hormones of the adrenal cortex were isolated, identified, and prepared by synthetic methods in small amounts. Subsequently, they were made commercially on a scale sufficiently large to permit a study of their physiological effects. Previous to this, Dr. Philip Hench, also at the Mayo Foundation, had observed that patients who had rheumatoid arthritis were sometimes relieved if they developed jaundice. In women, rheumatoid arthritis was sometimes relieved during pregnancy. When one of the hormones of the adrenal cortex was given to patients by Dr. Hench, the anti-inflammatory effect of the compound, cortisone, was discovered. It was then found that many other diseases of an inflammatory nature were relieved by cortisone. Although it was found later that cortisone, like insulin, acts only so long as it is given to the patient, and that it does not cure the disease, the discovery of the activity of cortisone was a great step forward. It has led to our modern knowledge of the hormones of the adrenal cortex and their uses in medicine. For their work, Kendall, Hench, and Reichstein jointly were given the Nobel Prize for Physiology and Medicine for 1950. Since his retirement to Princeton University, Kendall has continued his studies of the chemistry of the adrenal cortex.

Kendall received many awards and other honours, some of these (Lasker Award of the American Public Health Service, Passano Award of the Passano Foundation in San Francisco, and Page One Award of the Newspaper Guild of New York) jointly with Dr. Hench. On December 1915, he married Rebecca Kennedy; they have two children.

*Edward C. Kendall died on May 4, 1972.*

## PRIZE ACCEPTANCE SPEECH

*Edward C. Kendall's speech at the Nobel Banquet in Stockholm, December 10, 1950*

*Your Excellencies, Distinguished Guests, Ladies and Gentlemen:*

I wish to express my appreciation to the faculty of the Caroline Institute for the invitation to be with you tonight, not as a guest, but in the role of one of the participants.

The year 1950 marks the fiftieth anniversary of the establishment of the Nobel Prize and it is the good fortune of the recipients of the awards this year to be present on this memorable occasion. I hope you will not consider it trivial when I point out that the year 1950 also terminates fifty years of chemical investigation of the adrenal gland.

Epinephrine from the adrenal medulla was isolated in 1901. Interest in the adrenal cortex has been world wide and it is significant that Professor Reichstein from Switzerland and Doctor Hench and I from the United States are honored here tonight.

It is also significant that the award is for investigations carried out in the fields of both organic chemistry and clinical medicine. This fact illustrates the complex nature of the problem, for without the work of the chemist, the clinician could not advance beyond the stage of hypothesis, and without the clinician the contributions of the organic chemist could not come to fruition. Now the Caroline Institute has recognized this work and bestowed the Nobel Prize, the highest honor that can come to any man. Through the work of many investigators we now know that our material welfare depends in large part on the activity of the adrenal cortex and this knowledge, of itself, contributes to spiritual growth and freedom from superstition and fear. These most recent advances are in accord with the hope and vision of that forward looking man whose death is commemorated today - Alfred Nobel.

# MAX THEILER
## 1951

### INTRODUCTION

MAX THEILER was born on January 30, 1899, in Pretoria, South Africa, one of the four children of Sir Arnold and Emma (*née* Jegge) Theiler. His father was a well-known veterinary scientist. He attended local schools except for one year in Basle, Switzerland (his father was of Swiss origin), then went on to Rhodes University College, Grahamstown and the University of Capetown Medical School (1916-1918). He then went to England to study at St. Thomas' Hospital and at the London School of Tropical Medicine, receiving his medical degree in 1922. In the same year he became a Licentiate of the Royal College of Physicians and a Member of the Royal College of Surgeons.

In 1922 he joined the Department of Tropical Medicine at the Harvard Medical School, Boston, Massachusetts, first as an assistant, then being appointed instructor. In 1930 he joined the staff of the International Health Division of the Rockefeller Foundation, becoming, in 1951, Director of Laboratories of the Rockefeller Foundation's Division of Medicine and Public Health, New York.

His early work, at Harvard, dealt with amoebic dysentery and rat bite fever. He also worked on the problem of yellow fever, a subject in which he had become interested whilst still in London. This was to become his major interest. By 1927 he and his colleagues had proved that the cause of yellow fever was not a bacterium but a filterable virus. He also demonstrated that the disease could be readily transmitted to mice.

Previously, laboratory work on this topic had been done using monkeys as experimental animals; the use of mice enabled the cost of such research to be greatly reduced. In 1930, when he joined the Rockefeller Foundation, that body was engaged in a broad attack on the problem of yellow fever. Here, Theiler and his colleagues worked on vaccines against the disease and eventually developed a safe, standardized vaccine, 17D, one advantage of which was its ready adaptability to mass production.

His other work for the Institute has been connected with the causes and immunology of certain disorders which include Weil's disease. He has also been engaged in research on dengue fever and Japanese encephalitis. The problem of poliomyelitis has been of great interest to him and he discovered an apparently identical disorder in laboratory mice which is now sometimes called Theiler's disease (encephalomyelitis).

Dr. Theiler has been a contributor to two books, *Viral and Rickettsial Infections of Man* (1948) and *Yellow Fever* (1951). He has also written numerous papers in *The American Journal of Tropical Medicine* and *Annals of Tropical Medicine and Parasitology.*

Honours awarded to him include the Chalmer's Medal of the Royal Society of Tropical Medicine and Hygiene (London, 1939), the Flattery Medal (Harvard, 1945), and the Lasker Award of the Lasker Foundation (1949). He married Lillian Graham in 1928. They have one daughter.

*Max Theiler died on August 11, 1972.*

## PRIZE ACCEPTANCE SPEECH

*Max Theiler's speech at the Nobel Banquet in Stockholm, December 10, 1951*

*Your Majesty, Your Royal Highnesses, Ladies and Gentlemen.*

To have been considered worthy of receiving the Nobel Prize - the highest honor that any scientist can receive - gives me a feeling of great personal satisfaction. Such tangible evidence that my work has been considered of benefit to mankind is indeed very gratifying.

Apart from these personal feelings, I am glad that the Award has gone to someone working on yellow fever, for the conquest of this disease has been one of the great epics in medical history. It is barely fifty years ago that this disease was shown to be transmitted by a mosquito - knowledge gained by the use of human volunteers of whom several died. Surely this was one of the most glorious and heroic episodes ever recorded, but these deaths brought to an end further investigations. However, by the application of the knowledge thus gained, the devastating epidemics became a thing of the past, and the control of this disease in cities where for ages it had been prevalent, led the Rockefeller Foundation to undertake the ambitious program of attempting to eradicate yellow fever from the whole world. Just when it appeared that this program was about to be crowned with success in the Americas, it was discovered that yellow fever is primarily a disease of wild animals in the jungles, and thus an eternal potential danger. Old methods of control were inadequate and new ones had to be found.

The modern phase of yellow fever research commenced in 1928, when it was discovered that this disease could be transmitted to laboratory animals. I have had the good fortune to be associated with this great adventure since that time, and it has been a thrilling experience. Like the early one, this modern phase was not without danger, for many accidental infections and several deaths occurred. In spite of these, the work went on.

The study of yellow fever, in all its aspects, under the auspices of the Rockefeller Foundation, has been a magnificent example of international cooperation in which important advances were made by representatives in many countries on four continents. I like to feel that in honoring me you are honoring all the workers in the laboratory, field, and jungle who have contributed so much, often under conditions of hardship and danger, to our understanding of this disease. I would also like to feel that you are honoring the memory of those who gave their lives in gaining knowledge which was of inestimable value. They were truly martyrs of science, who died that others might live. And, finally, I would like to feel that in honoring me you are honoring the Rockefeller Foundation under whose auspices most of the modern work on yellow fever has been done - a gesture from one great foundation to another - both having the ideal of benefiting mankind throughout the world. I thank you.

# KONRAD BLOCH
## 1964

### INTRODUCTION

KONRAD E. BLOCH was born on 21st January 1912, in Neisse, Upper Silesia, then Germany, the son of Fritz Bloch and his wife Hedwig, née Striemer. He attended the elementary school and the Real gymnasium in the same city and in 1930 went to Munich to study chemistry at the Technische Hochschule.

For racial reasons his studies in Munich ended in 1934 after he had obtained the degree of Diplom-Ingenieur in Chemistry.

In 1936 Bloch was able to immigrate to the United States as he had long hoped. On advice by the late Max Bergmann and with the generous support of the Wallerstein Foundation, he entered the Department of Biochemistry, College of Physicians and Surgeons, Columbia University, where he became a graduate student under Hans T. Clarke. Research leading to the Ph.D. degree was completed in 1938.

In 1946 Bloch moved to the University of Chicago as Assistant Professor of Biochemistry. Appointments to Associate Professor and Professor followed in 1948 and 1950, respectively. At Chicago, in the Biochemistry Department headed by E. A. Evans Jr., the intellectual climate was stimulating and the conditions ideal for the development of young investigators. Work on cholesterol, biosynthesis was continued and progressed well with the aid of able and enthusiastic students.

In 1954 Bloch was appointed Higgins Professor of Biochemistry in the Department of Chemistry, Harvard University, and in 1968 he became Chairman of the Department. Apart from continuing research on various aspects of terpene and sterol biogenesis, he has become interested in the enzymatic formation of unsaturated fatty acids and more recently in various aspects of biochemical evolution.

Professor Bloch is a member of the American Chemical Society, National Academy of Sciences U. S., American Academy of Arts and Sciences, American Society of Biological Chemists, Harvey Society, American Philosophical Society, a honorary member of the Lombardy Academy of Sciences, and a Senior Fellow of the Australian Academy of Science. He was President of the American Society of Biological Chemists (1967), Chairman of the Section of Biochemistry, National Academy of Sciences (1966-1969), and Chairman of the National Committee for the International Union of Biochemistry (1968).

Dr. Bloch has been honored as recipient of the following medals and awards: Medal of the Sociëté de Chimie Biologique (1958), Fritzsche Award (American Chemical Society, 1964), Centennial Science Award (University of Notre Dame, 1965), Cardano Medal (Lombardy Academy of Sciences, 1965), Distinguished Service Award (University of Chicago School of Medicine, 1964), William Lloyd Evans Award (Ohio State University, 1968). He holds honorary doctor degrees from the universities of Uruguay (1966), Brazil (1966), Nancy (1966), Columbia University (1967) ,Technische Hochschule, Munich (1968), and Brandeis University (1970).

In 1941 Konrad Bloch married Lore Teutsch, a native of Munich. They have two children, Peter, and Susan.

*Konrad Bloch died on October 15, 2000.*

## PRIZE ACCEPTANCE SPEECH

*Konrad Bloch's speech at the Nobel Banquet in Stockholm, December 10, 1964*

*Your Majesties, Your Royal Highnesses, Your Excellencies, Ladies and Gentlemen:*

The last few weeks have been a time of great happiness, elation and pride for my family and me. We have looked forward excitedly to visiting Stockholm in anticipation of the events which have reached their highest point to-night. The warmth of your welcome and your hospitality has overwhelmed us and surpass by far what we had imagined.

At this moment I am above all conscious of the supreme way in which you are honoring me, deeply grateful to the Nobel Committee for having recognized my work and greatly pleased to be here, together with my friend Feodor Lynen.

I would not be among you to-night but for the mentors, colleagues and students who have guided and aided me throughout my scientific life. I wish I could name them all and tell you their contributions. More, however, than anyone else it was the late Rudolf Schoenheimer, a brilliant scholar and a man of infectious enthusiasm, who introduced me to the wonders of Biochemistry. Ever since, I have been happy to have chosen science as my career, and, to borrow a phrase of Jacques Barzun, have felt that "Science is, in the best and strictest sense, glorious entertainment". To give expression to my feelings at this moment I can say no more than:

"Tack så mycket för allt."

# EARL W. SUTHERLAND, JR.
## 1971

### INTRODUCTION

EARL WILBUR SUTHERLAND, Jr. American pharmacologist and physiologist who was awarded the 1971 Nobel Prize for Physiology or Medicine for isolating cyclic adenosine monophosphate (cyclic AMP) and demonstrating its involvement in numerous metabolic processes that occur in animals. Sutherland graduated from Washburn College (Topeka, Kansas) in 1937 and received his M.D. degree from Washington University Medical School (St. Louis, Missouri) in 1942.

After serving in the U.S. Army during World War II, he joined the faculty of Washington University. In 1953 he became chairman of the department of pharmacology at Western Reserve University (now Case Western Reserve University) in Cleveland, Ohio, where in 1956 he discovered cyclic AMP.

In 1963 Sutherland became a professor of physiology at Vanderbilt University (Nashville, Tennessee), and from 1973 until his death he was a member of the faculty of the University of Miami Medical School.

### PRIZE ACCEPTANCE SPEECH

*Earl W. Sutherland's speech at the Nobel Banquet in Stockholm, December 10, 1971*

*Your Royal Highnesses, Ladies and Gentlemen,*

It is indeed an honour to me and a pleasure to receive this award. I believe we all realize the honour and pleasure that a scientist receives with this award.

I hadn't realized however how important this award is to others. A flood of telegrams and letters arrived after the announcement mostly from the USA but many from around the globe. These were positive and friendly letters, hopeful for medical research. What I liked especially was that many young people wrote me. One, eleven years old wanted to know the procedure for winning such a prize.

Now I mention this response for a reason. I am fully convinced that medical research can offer one a happy and productive life. And if one has a little viking spirit he can explore the world and people as no one else can do. The whole medical research area is wide open for exploration and I believe soon for productive application.

My experience with this award is that it does make me happy, but more importantly it stimulates many others including the young. We need much more medical research and this helps.

# ALLAN M. CORMACK
# 1979

## INTRODUCTION

ALLAN MACLEOD CORMACK[mukloud´, cOr´muk], 1924–98, American physicist, b. Johannesburg, South Africa. After studying at the Univ. of Cape Town (B.S. physics, 1944, M.S. crystallography, 1945), Cambridge, and Harvard, Cormack became a professor at Tufts Univ. in 1958. His interest in X-ray technology led him to develop the theoretical foundations that made computerized axial tomography (CAT) scanning possible.

He published his results in two papers in 1963–64, but these generated little interest until the first CAT scan machine, built under the leadership of Godfrey Hounsfield, was introduced in 1972. For their independent efforts, Cormack and Hounsfield shared the 1979 Nobel Prize in Physiology or Medicine.

## PRIZE ACCEPTANCE SPEECH

*Allan M. Cormack's speech at the Nobel Banquet, December 10, 1979*

*Your Majesties, Your Royal Highnesses, Ladies and Gentlemen,*

Godfrey Hounsfield has asked me to speak for both of us.

We would most respectfully request Your Majesty to convey to the Nobel Foundation and the Nobel Assembly of Karolinska Institutet our intense gratitude for the honour which they have done us by awarding us the Nobel Prize for medicine and physiology.

There is irony in this award, since neither Hounsfield nor I is a physician. In fact it is not much of an exaggeration to say that what Hounsfield and I know about medicine and physiology could be written on a small prescription form!

While there is irony in the award, there is also hope that even in these days of increasing specialization there is a unity in the human experience, a unity clearly known to Alfred Nobel by the broad spectrum of his awards. I think that he would have been pleased to know that an engineer and a physicist, each in his own way, have contributed just a little to the advancement of medicine.

# SUSUMU TONEGAWA
## 1987

### INTRODUCTION

SUSUMU TONEGAWA was born at Nagoya in Japan and educated at Kyoto University and the University of California, San Diego. He worked at the Basle Institute for Immunology from 1971 and in 1981 was appointed professor of biology at the Center for Cancer Research and Department of Biology of the Massachusetts Institute of Technology. Working at Basle in collaboration with Niels Jerne and Nobumichi Hozumi, Tonegawa revealed how the immune system is capable of generating the enormous diversity of antibodies required so that whatever the nature of the invading organism or 'foreign' tissue a suitable antibody is available to bind specifically to it.

This implies that the immune system's antibody-producing cells – the B-lymphocytes – can potentially manufacture billions of different antibodies; yet, even in humans, these cells carry only about 100,000 genes on their chromosomes.

Working with mouse cells, Tonegawa showed that during the development of the antibody-producing cell, the genes coding for antibody are shuffled at random, so that in the mature cell a cluster of functional genes is formed specific to that cell. Each individual mature cell thus produces its own specific antibody. This potential diversity is amplified by the fact that each antibody molecule comprises four protein chains, all with a highly variable terminal region. Hence the diversity of antibodies is a consequence of the huge numbers of lymphocytes present in the body, each with its own combination of functional antibody-producing genes. In recognition of the significance of his discovery Tonegawa was awarded the 1987 Nobel Prize for physiology or medicine.

## PRIZE ACCEPTANCE SPEECH

*Susumu Tonegawa's speech at the Nobel Banquet, December 10, 1987*

*Your Majesties, Your Royal Highnesses, Ladies and Gentlemen,*

I have great difficulties in finding proper words to express my heartfelt gratitude to those in the Committee and Assembly who considered my work worthy of this ultimate recognition. It is, indeed, a high honor that you have bestowed upon me today.

My scientific career has developed on three continents: Asia, Europe and North America. A quarter of a century ago as a student at the University of Kyoto in Japan, I started my career as a scientist, inspired by the operon theory of François Jacob and Jacques Monod. At the suggestion of Professor Itaru Watanabe and with his help I left Japan at the age of twenty-three to pursue graduate study at the University of California at San Diego. Seven years later, following the suggestion of Dr. Renato Dulbecco, I left the United States to embark on research in immunology at the Basel Institute for Immunology in Basel, Switzerland. This unique research Institute had recently been established by the Hoffmann LaRoche Company to allow pioneering immunologists from around the world to carry out basic research. Under the directorship of Professor Niels Kaj Jerne, the Institute conducted its work in an atmosphere of freedom and cooperation. It was in this great Institute that I and my colleagues carried out the research on antibody genes, that is being recognized today by the Nobel Assembly. In 1981, after ten years in Basel, I returned to the United States to continue my research on the immune system at the Center for Cancer Research of the Massachusetts Institute of Technology where Director Salvador E. Luria provided me with an excellent laboratory.

Yesterday during the tour of the Nobel Foundation I had the opportunity to view the original of Alfred Nobel's will that led to the establishment of these first truly international prizes. I could not help feeling very proud when I read the passage in which Mr. Nobel emphasized his wish to have these prizes bestowed upon the most worthy without consideration of nationality. I too have always believed that the community of science recognizes no national boundaries, and I have been practicing this belief throughout my career.

On this very special occasion I wish to extend my sincere gratitude to all my coworkers, technical assistants and secretaries. Without their interest and devotion, the work recognized by the Nobel Assembly could not have been accomplished. Slutligen vill jag tacka det svenska folket for dess storartade gästfrihet.

# STANLEY B. PRUSINER
## 1997

### INTRODUCTION

STANLEY B. PRUSINER won the 1997 Nobel Prize in Physiology or Medicine for his ground-breaking, yet controver-sial, work on a type of protein particle, a prion, thathe hypothesized was responsible for a number of fatal neurodegenera-tive disorders, including Creutzfeldt-Jakob disease (CJD) and mad cow disease.

Prusiner was born on May 28, 1942, in Des Moines, Iowa. He earned his B.A., *cum laude*, at the University of Pennsylvania, in 1964, and then went onto receive an M.D. in 1968 from the same university.

Prusiner combined a zeal for research with a disarming political sense to wingrants for the study of such diseases, including CJD, scrapie, kuru, fatal familial insomnia, and bovine spongiform encephalopathy (BSE), or mad cow disease. Over three decades, he managed to gain funding totaling 56 million dollars from the National Institutes of Health (NIH).

Expanding on work by British researchers as well as the NIH's Rocky MountainLaboratories, which had shown similarities between kuru and scrapie, Prusinerset up a research team at UCSF employing ultimately a quarter million mice infected with diseased brain matter in an attempt to isolate the infective agent in neurodegenerative diseases. Such research was laborious and time-consuming, for the incubation period in mice took upwards of 200 days. Early breakthroughs occurred when Prusiner switched from mice to hamsters, as the onset of illness in those animals would occur twice as fast. By 1981,

Prusiner was able to conclude that a protein was the causative agent in these brain diseases, and he dubbed this agent the prion.

By 1992, Prusiner's research more clearly demonstrated the nature of the interaction between prion proteins. Prusiner showed that when the gene encoding for the prion protein in mice was destroyed, such mice (called prion knock-outmice) proved resistant to the diseases when injected with preparations of disease-causing prion protein.

The diseases which Prusiner studied are life-threatening to only a tiny fraction of the world's population—the annual death toll of CJD in the United States annually, for example, is about 225, less than the number of traffic fatalities in two days. However, as the Nobel committee noted, Prusiner's research could lead to new therapies for a larger array of neurological disorders such as Alzheimer's and Parkinson's disease, which may or may notbe caused by protein-based infective agents. In the case of prion-based diseases, Prusiner has suggested gene therapy to curtail the production of prionproteins and thus eliminate the spread of such diseases, as was done with hisprion knock-out mice.

## PRIZE ACCEPTANCE SPEECH

*Stanley B. Prusiner's speech at the Nobel Banquet, December 10, 1996*

King Carl Gustaf, Queen Silvia, Distinguished Guests,

Tonight's awarding of the Nobel Prizes and this elegant Banquet are a grand celebration of science and culture. These events honor the vision, courage, and wisdom of Alfred Nobel, a superb scientist in his own right.

And they honor the Swedish people's uncommon sense of commitment to fulfill the enlightened wishes of Alfred Nobel - the Nobel Prizes have truly become important benchmarks in the history of science.

But the Nobel Prizes are much more than awards to scholars, they are a celebration of civilization, of mankind, and of what makes humans unique - that is their intellect from which springs creativity. I continue to be delightfully surprised by the joy, excitement, and happiness that so many of my friends and colleagues have felt when they learned of this year's Nobel Prize in Medicine; moreover, many of these friends are nonscientists who hail from many parts of our planet.

People often ask me why I persisted in doing research on a subject that was so controversial. I frequently respond by telling them that only a few scientists are granted the great fortune to pursue topics that are so new and different that only a small number of people can grasp the meaning of such discoveries initially. I am one of those genuinely lucky scientists who was handed a special opportunity to work on such a problem - that of prions.

Because our results were so novel, my colleagues and I had great difficulty convincing other scientists of the veracity of our findings and communicating to lay people the importance of work that seemed so esoteric! As more and more compelling data accumulated, many scientists became convinced. But it was the "mad cow" epidemic in Britain and the likely transmission of bovine prions to humans producing a fatal brain illness called Creutzfeldt-Jakob disease that introduced prions to the public. Yet the principles of prion biology are still so new that some scientists and most laymen, including the press, still have considerable difficulty grasping the most fundamental concepts.

Being a scientist is a special privilege: for it brings the opportunity to be creative, the passionate quest for answers to nature's most precious secrets, and the warm friendships of many valued colleagues. Collaborations extend far beyond the scientific achievements, no matter how great the accomplishments might be, the rich friendships which have no national borders are treasured even more.

Besides scientific achievement, the Nobel Prizes honor the scientific process. In science, each new result, sometimes quite surprising, heralds a step forward and allows one to discard some hypotheses, even though one or two of these might have been highly favored. No matter how new and revolutionary the findings may be, as data accumulates, even the skeptical scholars eventually become convinced except for a few who will always remain resistant. Indeed, the story of prions is truly an odyssey that has taken us from heresy to orthodoxy.

Lastly, we celebrate on the occasion of these Nobel Prizes,

the triumph of science over prejudice. The wondrous tools of modern science allowed my colleagues and me to demonstrate that prions exist and that they are responsible for an entirely new principle of infection.

Tack så mycket!

# SIR PETER MANSFIELD
# 2003

## INTRODUCTION

SIR PETER MANSFIELD was born on 9 October 1933, Nottingham, England.

Won the Nobel Prize for medicine in 2003 for his pioneering work with magnetic resonance imaging (MRI).

Mansfield left school aged 15 and worked as a printer before joining the army. He only entered academic life after studying part-time to complete his school exams. He then earned a bachelor degree and doctorate at the University of London. After a spell in the United States he started work at the University of Nottingham, eventually becoming Emeritus Professor of Physics there.

Mansfield played a key role in the development of MRI, a scanning technique that uses a strong magnetic field to reveal internal organs and other tissues in extraordinary detail. Mansfield showed how the signals emitted by the body in response to the magnetic field could be mathematically analysed to produce a clear image. He also demonstrated how to achieve extremely fast imaging.

MRI is important for medical diagnosis, treatment and follow-up. In many cases it has eliminated the need for surgery. Worldwide, more than 60 million investigations are performed each year using MRI.

Mansfield was elected Fellow of the Royal Society, London, in 1987 and received a knighthood in 1993.

## PRIZE ACCEPTANCE SPEECH

*Sir Peter Mansfield's speech at the Nobel Banquet, December 10, 2003*

*Your Majesties, Your Royal Highnesses, Honoured Laureates, Ladies and Gentlemen:-*

The sparkle, the jubilation, the sheer grandeur of the Nobel Fest, is a most splendid occasion in which we, by your grace, have been invited to participate. We feel greatly honoured to be here and especially honoured to receive the Awards for our work in magnetic resonance imaging (MRI).

But there is another, darker side to our work. This side is expressed in the suffering and mental anguish associated with those afflicted with devastating illness. It is therefore all the more rewarding for us when someone takes a moment to write thanking us for the peace of mind felt by them in revealing their problem through MRI. In many cases accurate diagnosis together with surgical and/or drug intervention indicates a brighter future beyond the illness.

Of the many letters received recently what comes through in much of the correspondence is the strong sense of relief at knowing the details of their illness and the hope inspired by the rigorous evaluation of their problem using MRI.

Many patients offer their profuse thanks that such machines now exist. A few comment on the claustrophobic affects of tight confinement, while some people have commented on the rather high level of acoustic noise that occurs during the scanning process. They will all be pleased to know that these problems are not being ignored but rather, are the subject of intensive effort in continuing research and development.

We now wish to express our deep gratitude for the honours bestowed on us this day and we offer our thanks for the opportunity to be here present.

Thank you.

# OLIVER SMITHIES
# 2007

## INTRODUCTION

OLIVER SMITHIES, born 1925 in Great Britain, US citizen, PhD in Biochemistry 1951, Oxford University, UK. Dr. Oliver Smithies, Excellence professor of pathology and laboratory medicine at the University of North Carolina at Chapel Hill School of Medicine, is a co-recipient of this year's Nobel Prize in physiology or medicine. He attended a high school for bright students and won a scholarship to Oxford University. He earned a bachelor of arts degree (first- class honors) in physiology from Oxford in 1946, and he went on to earn his master's degree and doctorate in biochemistry from Oxford in 1951.

The Nobel Foundation today announced that Smithies, along with Mario R. Capecchi of the University of Utah's Howard Hughes Medical Institute and Sir Martin J. Evans of the United Kingdom, will share this year's Nobel Prize "for their discoveries of principles for introducing specific gene modifications in mice by the use of embryonic stem cells."

Smithies received the call from Stockholm at his home in Chapel Hill at 5 a.m. "I now have a peaceful sense of the rounding off of a scientific life," Smithies later said.

## PRIZE ACCEPTANCE SPEECH

*Oliver Smithies' speech at the Nobel Banquet, 10 December 2007*

*Your Majesties, Your Royal Highnesses, Your Excellencies, Ladies and Gentlemen.*

The three of us (Mario Capecchi, Martin Evans and myself) thank the Nobel Assembly at Karolinska Institutet and the Nobel Foundation for honoring us today. And we thank our students and collaborators, whose help was indispensable in our research. But we also acknowledge an *older debt – to our teachers* – which I want to illustrate with three of mine.

The first, Dr. G.E. Brown, taught mathematics at Heath Grammar school in Halifax, England. "Oddy" Brown, as we called him, was a poor disciplinarian, and not much liked. But *he loved mathematics, and the calculus,* and he conveyed this to at least one student – *me*!

The second, Field Morey, is a distinguished flight instructor. He taught me to fly 30 years ago, a difficult task because I was over 50 years of age! But *he taught me something more important than flying* – namely, that *it is possible to overcome fear with knowledge*!

This same lesson applies to scientists – *the fear of failing* – which many scientists have when trying something new – *can be overcome* – in the same way – *with knowledge.*

The third of my teachers is Dr. A. G. ("Sandy") Ogston. He was my tutor as an undergraduate at Balliol College, Oxford University, and later oversaw my change from medical school to graduate school in order to take up research. Sandy was an extraordinary scientist, and a dedicated teacher. And he *conveyed to his students a view of science,* which I quote in closing:

*"For science is more than the search for truth, more than a challenging game, more than a profession. It is a life that a diversity of people lead together, in the closest proximity, a school for social living. We are members one of another."**

* A.G.Ogston, Australian Biochem. Soc. Annual Lecture, *Search,* Vol.1, No.2, August, 1970.

# CHEMISTRY

## MARIE CURIE
## 1911

### INTRODUCTION

MARIE CURIE, née Marie Sklodowska *(sklaw DAWF skah)* was born November 7, 1867 in Warsaw, Poland. She would become famous for her research into radioactivity, and was the first woman to win a Nobel prize.

Marie Curie grew up in a family that valued education. As a young woman she went to Paris to study mathematics, chemistry and physics. She began studying at the Sorbonne in 1891, and was the first woman to teach there. She adopted the French spelling of her name (Marie) and also met Pierre Curie, who taught physics at University of Paris. Marie and Pierre soon married, and teamed up to conduct research on radioactive substances. They found that the uranium ore, or pitchblende, contained much more radioactivity than could be explained solely by the uranium content.

The Curie's began a search for the source of the radioactivity and discovered two highly radioactive elements, "radium" and "polonium." The Curie's won the 1903 Nobel prize for physics for their discovery. They shared the award with another French physicist, Antoine Henri Bacquerel, who had discovered natural radioactivity. In 1906 Pierre, overworked and weakened by his prolonged exposure to radiation, died when he was run over by a horse drawn wagon.

Madame Curie continued her work on radioactive elements and won the 1911 Nobel prize for chemistry for isolating radium and studying its chemical properties. In 1914 she helped found the Radium Institute in Paris, and was the Institute's first director. When the first world war broke out, Madame Curie thought X-rays would help to locate bullets and facilitate surgery. It was also important not to move the wounded, so she invented X-ray vans and trained 150 female attendants.

On July 4, 1934, at the age of 67 Madame Curie died of leukemia (aplastic pernicious anemia), thought to have been brought on by exposure to the high levels of radiation involved in her research. After her death the Radium Institute was rename the Curie Institute in her honor.

## PRIZE ACCEPTANCE SPEECH

### *Radium and the New Concepts in Chemistry*

Some 15 years ago the radiation of uranium was discovered by Henri Becquerel[1], and two years later the study of this phenomenon was extended to other substances, first by me, and then by Pierre Curie and myself[2]. This study rapidly led us to the discovery of new elements, the radiation of which, while being analogous with that of uranium, was far more intense. All the elements emitting such radiation I have termed *radioactive*, and the new property of matter revealed in this emission has thus received the name *radioactivity*. Thanks to this discovery of new, very powerful radioactive substances, particularly radium, the study of radioactivity progressed with marvellous rapidity: Discoveries followed each other in rapid succession, and it was obvious that a new science was in course of development. The Swedish Academy of Sciences was kind enough to celebrate the birth of this science by awarding the Nobel Prize for Physics to the first workers in the field, Henri Becquerel, Pierre Curie and Marie Curie (1903).

From that time onward numerous scientists devoted themselves to the study of radioactivity. Allow me to recall to you one of them who, by the certainty of his judgement, and the boldness of his hypotheses and through the many investigations carried out by him and his pupils, has succeeded not only in increasing our knowledge but also in classifying it with great clarity; he has provided a backbone for the new science, in the form of a very precise theory admirably suited to the study of the phenomena. I am happy to recall that Rutherford came to Stockholm in 1908 to receive the Nobel Prize as a well-deserved reward for his work.

Far from halting, the development of the new science has constantly continued to follow an upward course. And now, only 15 years after Becquerel's discovery, we are face to face with a whole world of new phenomena belonging to a field which, despite its close connexion with the fields of physics and chemistry, is particularly well-defined. In this field the importance of radium from, the viewpoint of general theories has been decisive. The history of the discovery and the isolation of this substance has furnished proof of my hypothesis *that radioactivity is an atomic property of matter and can provide a means of seeking new elements.* This hypothesis has led to present-day theories of radioactivity, according to which we can predict with certainty the existence of about 30 new elements which we cannot generally either isolate or characterize by chemical methods. We also assume that these elements undergo atomic transformations, and the most direct proof in favour of this theory is provided by the experimental fact of the formation of the chemically defined element *helium* starting from the chemically-defined element *radium.*

Viewing the subject from this angle, it can be said that the task of isolating radium is the corner-stone of the edifice of the science of radioactivity. Moreover, radium remains the most useful and powerful tool in radioactivity laboratories. I believe that it is because of these considerations that the Swedish Academy of Sciences has done me the very great honour of awarding me this year's Nobel Prize for Chemistry.

It is therefore my task to present to you radium in particular as a new chemical element, and to leave aside the description of the many radioactive phenomena which have already been described in the Nobel Lectures of H. Becquerel, P. Curie and E. Rutherford.

Before broaching the subject of this lecture, I should like to recall that the discoveries of radium and of polonium were made by Pierre Curie in collaboration with me. We are also indebted to Pierre Curie for basic research in the field of radioactivity, which has been carried out either alone, in collaboration with his pupils.

The chemical work aimed at isolating radium in the state of the pure salt, and at characterizing it as a new element, was carried out specially by me, but it is intimately connected with our common work. I thus feel that I interpret correctly the intention of the Academy of Sciences in assuming that the award of this high distinction to me is motivated by this common work and thus pays homage to the memory of Pierre Curie.

I will remind you at the outset that one of the most important properties of the radioactive elements is that of ionizing the air in their vicinity (Becquerel). When a uranium compound is placed on a metal plate A situated opposite another plate B and a difference in potential is maintained between the plates A and B, an electric current is set up between these plates; this current can be measured with accuracy under suitable conditions and will serve as a measure of the activity of the substance. The conductivity imparted to the air can be ascribed to ionization produced by the rays emitted by the uranium compounds.

In 1897, using this method of measurement, I undertook a study of the radiation of uranium compounds, and soon extended this study to other substances, with the aim of finding out whether radiation of this type occurs in other elements. I found in this way that of the other elements known, only the compounds of thorium behave like the compounds of uranium.

I was struck by the fact that the activity of uranium and thorium compounds appears to be *an atomic property of the element uranium and of the element thorium.* Chemical compounds and mixtures containing uranium and thorium are active in direct proportion to the amount of these metals contained in them. The activity is not destroyed by either physical changes of state or chemical transformations.

I measured the activity of a number of minerals; all of them that appear to be radioactive always contain uranium or thorium. But an unexpected fact was noted: certain minerals (pitchblende, chalcolite, autunite) had a greater activity than might be expected on the basis of their uranium or thorium content. Thus, certain pitchblendes containing 75% of uranium oxide are about four times as radioactive as this oxide. Chalcolite (crystallized phosphate of copper and uranium) is about twice as radioactive as uranium. This conflicted with views which held that no mineral should be more radioactive than metallic uranium. To explain this point I prepared synthetic chalcolite from pure products, and obtained crystals, whose activity was completely consistent with their uranium content; this activity is about half that of uranium.

I then thought that the greater activity of the natural minerals might be determined by the presence of a small quantity of a highly-radioactive material, different from uranium, thorium and the elements known at present. It also occurred to me that if this was the case I might be able to extract this substance from the mineral by the ordinary methods of chemical analysis. Pierre Curie and I at once carried out this research, hoping that the proportion of the new element might reach several per cent. In reality the proportion of the hypothetical element was far lower and it took several years to show unequivocally that pitchblende contains at least one highly-radioactive material which is a new element in the sense that chemistry attaches to the term.

We were thus led to create a new method of searching for new elements, *a method based on radioactivity considered as an atomic property of matter*. Each chemical separation is followed by a measurement of the activity of the products obtained, and in this way it is possible to determine how the active substance behaves from the chemical viewpoint. This method has come into general application, and is similar in some ways to spectral analysis. Because of the wide variety of radiation emitted, the method could be perfected and extended, so that it makes it possible, not only to discover radioactive materials, but also to distinguish them from each other with certainty.

It was also found in using the method being considered, that it was in fact possible to concentrate the activity by chemical methods. We found that pitchblende contains at least two radioactive materials, one of which, accompanying bismuth, has been given the name *polonium*, while the other, paired with barium, has been called *radium*.

Other radioactive elements have been discovered since: actinium (Debierne), radiothorium and mesothorium (Hahn), ionium (Boltwood), etc.

We were convinced that the materials which we had discovered were new chemical elements. This conviction was based solely on the atomic nature of radioactivity. But at first, from the chemical viewpoint, it was as if our substances had been, the one pure bismuth, and the other pure barium. It was vital to show that the radioactive property was connected with traces of elements that were neither bismuth nor barium. To do that the hypothetical elements had to be isolated. In the case of radium isolation was completely successful but required several years of unremitting effort. Radium in the pure salt form is a substance the manufacture of which has now been industrialized; for no other new radioactive substance have such positive results been obtained.

The radiferous minerals are being subjected to very keen study because the presence of radium lends them considerable value. They are identifiable either by the electrometric method, or very simply by the impression they produce on a photographic plate. The best radium mineral is the pitchblende from St. Joachimsthal (Austria) which has for a long time been processed to yield uranium salts. After extraction of the latter, the mineral leaves a residue which contains radium and polonium. We have normally used this residue as our raw material.

The first treatment consists in extracting the radiferous barium and the bismuth containing the polonium. This treatment, which was first performed in the laboratory on several kilograms of raw material (as many as 20 kg) had then to be undertaken in a factory owing to the need to process thousands of kilograms. Actually, we gradually learned from experience that the radium is contained in the raw material in the proportion of a few decigrams per ton. About 10 to 20 kg crude barium sulphate containing radium are extracted from one ton of residue. The activity of these sulphates is even then 30 to 60 times greater than that of uranium. These sulphates are purified and converted to chlorides. In the mixture of barium and radium chlorides the radium is present only in the proportion of about 3 parts per 100,000. In the radium industry in France a much lower grade mineral is most often used and the proportion indicated is far lower still. To separate the radium from the barium I have used a method of fractional crystallization of the chloride (the bromide can also be used). The radium salt, less soluble than the barium salt, becomes concentrated in the crystals. Fractionation is a lengthy, methodical operation which gradually eliminates the barium. To obtain a very pure salt I have had to perform several thousands of crystallizations. The progress of the fractionation is monitored by activity measurements.

A first proof that the element radium existed was furnished by spectral analysis. The spectrum of a chloride enriched by crystallization exhibited a new line which Demarcay attributed to the new element. As the activity became more concentrated, the new line increased in intensity and other lines appeared while the barium spectrum became at the same time less pronounced. When the purity is very high the barium spectrum is scarcely visible.

I have repeatedly determined the average atomic weight of the metal in the salt subjected to spectral analysis. The method used was the one consisting in determining the chlorine content in the form of silver chloride in a known amount of the anhydrous chloride. I have found that this method gives very good results even with quite small amounts of substance (0.1 to 0.5 g), provided a very fast balance is used to avoid the absorption of water by the alkaline-earth salt during the weighings. The atomic weight increases with the enrichment of the radium as indicated by the spectrum. The successive atomic weights obtained were: 138; 146; 174; 225; 226.45. This last value was determined in 1907 with 0.4 g of very pure radium salt. The results of a number of determinations are, 226.62; 226.31; 226.42. These have been confirmed by more recent experiments.

The preparation of pure radium salts and the determination of the atomic weight of radium have proved positively that radium is a new element and have enabled a definite position to be assigned to it. Radium is the higher homologue of barium in the family of alkaline-earth metals; it has been entered in Mendeleev's table in the corresponding column, on the row containing uranium and thorium. The radium spectrum is very precisely known. These very clear-cut results for radium have convinced chemists and justified the establishment of the new science of radioactive substances.

In chemical terms radium differs little from barium; the salts of these two elements are isomorphic, while those of radium are usually less soluble than the barium salts. It is very interesting to note that strong radioactivity of radium involves no chemical anomalies and that the chemical properties are actually those which correspond to the position in the Periodic System indicated by its atomic weight. The radioactivity of radium in solid salts is ca. 5

million times greater than that of an equal weight of uranium. Owing to this activity its salts are spontaneously luminous. I also wish to recall that radium gives rise to a continuous liberation of energy which can be measured as heat, being about 118 calories per gram of radium per hour.

Radium has been isolated in the metallic state (M. Curie and A. Debierne, 1910). The method used consisted in distilling under very pure hydrogen the amalgam of radium formed by the electrolysis of a chloride solution using a mercury cathode. One decigram only of salt was treated and consequently considerable difficulties were involved. The metal obtained melts at about 700°C, above which temperature it starts to volatilize. Is it very unstable in the air and decomposes water vigorously.

The radioactive properties of the metal are exactly the ones that can be forecast on the assumption that the radioactivity of the salts is an atomic property of the radium which is unaffected by the state of combination. It was of real importance to corroborate this point as misgivings had been voiced by those to whom the atomic hypothesis of radioactivity was still not evident.

Although radium has so far only been obtained in very small amounts, it is nevertheless true to say, in conclusion, that it is a perfectly defined and already well-studied chemical element.

Unfortunately, the same cannot be stated for polonium, for which nevertheless considerable effort has already been spent. The stumbling block here is the fact that the proportion of polonium in the mineral is about 5,000 times smaller than that of radium.

Before theoretical evidence was available from which to forecast this proportion, I had conducted several extremely laborious operations to concentrate polonium and in this way had secured products with very high activity without being able to arrive at definite results as in the case of radium. The difficulty is heightened by the fact that polonium disintegrates spontaneously, disappearing by half in a period of 140 days. We now know that radium has not an infinite life either, but the rate of disappearance is far less (it disappears by half in 2,000 years). With our facilities we can scarcely hope to determine the atomic weight of polonium because theory foresees that a rich mineral can contain only a few hundredths of a milligram per ton, but we can hope to observe its spectrum. The operation of concentrating polonium, as I shall point out later, is, moreover, a problem of great theoretical interest.

Recently, in collaboration with Debierne, I undertook to treat several tons of residues from uranium mineral with a view to preparing polonium. Initially conducted in the factory, then in the laboratory, this treatment finally yielded a few milligrams of substance about 50 times more active than an equal weight of pure radium. In the spectrum of the substance some new lines could be observed which appear attributable to polonium and of which the most important has the wavelength 4170.5 Å. According to the atomic hypothesis of radioactivity, the polonium spectrum should disappear at the same time as the activity and this fact can be confirmed experimentally, I have so far considered radium and polonium only as chemical substances. I have shown how the fundamental hypothesis which states that radioactivity is an atomic property of the substance has led to the discovery of new chemical elements. I shall now describe how the scope of this hypothesis has been greatly enlarged by the considerations and experimental facts which resulted in establishing the theory of atomic radioactive transformations.

The starting-point of this theory must be sought in the considerations of the source of the energy involved in the phenomena of radioactivity. This energy becomes manifest as an emission of rays which produce thermal, electrical and light phenomena. As the emission occurs spontaneously without any known cause of excitation, various hypotheses have been advanced to account for the liberation of energy. One of the hypotheses put forward at the beginning of our research by Pierre Curie and myself consisted in assuming that the radiation is an emission of matter accompanied by a loss in weight of the active substances and that the energy is taken from the substance itself whose evolution is not yet completes and which undergoes an atomic transformation. This hypothesis, which at first could only be enunciated together with other equally valid theories, has attained dominant importance and finally asserted itself in our minds owing to a body of experimental evidence which substantiated it. This evidence is essentially the following: A series of radioactive phenomena exists in which radioactivity appears to be tied up to matter in an imponderable quantity, the radiation moreover not being permanent but disappearing more or less rapidly with time. Such are polonium, radioactive emanations and deposits of induced radioactivity.

It has been established moreover in certain cases that the radioactivity observed increases with time. This is what happens in the case of freshly prepared radium, of the emanation freshly introduced into the measuring apparatus, of thorium deprived of thorium X, etc.

A careful study of these phenomena has shown that a very satisfactory general explanation can be given by assuming that each time a decrease of radioactivity is observed there is a destruction of radioactive matter, and that each time an increase of activity is observed, there is a production of radioactive matter. The radiations which disappear and appear are, besides, of very varied nature and it is admitted that every kind of rays determined can serve to characterize a substance which is its source, and appears and disappears with it.

As radioactivity is in addition a property which is essentially atomic, the production or the destruction of a distinct type of radioactivity corresponds to a production or a destruction of atoms of a radioactive substance.

Finally, if it is supposed that radioactive energy is a phenomenon which is borrowed from atomic transformation, it can be deduced from this that every radioactive substance undergoes such a transformation, even though it appears to us to be invariable. Transformation in this case is only very slow and this is what takes place in the case of radium or uranium.

The theory I have just summarized is the work of Rutherford and Soddy, which they have called *theory of atomic disintegration*. By applying this theory it can be concluded that a primary radioactive substance such as radium undergoes a series of atomic transmutations by virtue of which the atom of radium gives birth to a train of atoms of smaller and smaller weights, since a stable state cannot be attained as long as the atom formed is radioactive. Stability can only be attained by inactive matter.

From this point of view one of the most brilliant triumphs of the theory is the prediction that the gas helium, always present in radioactive minerals, can represent one of the end-products of the evolution of radium, and that it is in the form of alpha rays that the helium atoms which are formed when radium atoms distintegrate are discharged. Now, the production of helium by radium has been proved by the experiments of Ramsay and Soddy, and it cannot now be contested that the perfectly defined chemical element, radium, gives rise to the formation of another equally defined element - helium. Moreover, the investigations done by Rutherford and his students have proved that the alpha particles emitted by radium with an electric charge are also to be found in the form of helium gas in the space where they have been recovered.

I must remark here that the bold interpretation of the relationship existing between radium and helium rests entirely upon the certitude that radium has the same claim to be a chemical element as have all the other known elements, and that there can be no question of regarding it to be a molecular combination of helium with another element. This shows how fundamental in these circumstances has been the work carried out to prove the chemical individuality of radium, and it can also be seen in what way the hypothesis of the atomic nature of radioactivity and the theory of radioactive transformations have led to the experimental discovery of a first clearly-established example of atomic transmutation. This is a fact the significance of which cannot escape anyone, and one which incontestably marks an epoch from the point of view of chemists.

Considerable work, guided by the theory of radioactive transformations, has led to approximately 30 new radioactive elements being envisaged, classified in 4 series according to the primary substance: these series are uranium, radium, thorium and actinium. The uranium and radium series can, in fact, be combined, for it seems to be proved that radium is a derivative of uranium. In the radium series the last known radioactive body is polonium, the production of which by radium is now a proven fact. It is likely that the actinium series is related to that of radium.

We have seen that helium gas is one of the products of radium distintegration. The helium atoms are detached from those of radium and its derivatives during the course of the transformation. It is supposed that after the departure of four atoms of helium, the radium atom yields one atom of polonium; the departure of a fifth helium atom determines the formation of an inactive body with an atomic weight believed to be equal to 206 (20 units below that of radium).

According to Rutherford this final element is nothing more than lead, and this supposition is now being subjected to experimental verification in my laboratory. The production of helium from polonium has been directly proved by Debierne.

The relatively large amount of polonium prepared by Curie and Debierne has allowed an important study to be undertaken. This consists in counting a large number of alpha particles emitted by polonium and in collecting and measuring the corresponding volume of helium. Since each particle is a helium atom, the number of helium atoms is thus found which occupy a given volume and have a given weight. It can therefore allow us to deduce, in a general way, the number of molecules in a grammolecule. This number, known as Avogadro's constant, is of great importance. Experiments conducted on polonium have supplied a first value for this number, which is in good agreement with the values obtained by other methods. The enumeration of alpha particles is done by an electrometric method due to Rutherford; this method has been brought to perfection by means of a photographic recording apparatus.

Recent investigations have shown that potassium and rubidium emit a very feeble radiation, similar to the beta radiation of uranium and radium. We do not yet know whether we should regard these substances as true radioactive bodies, i.e. bodies in the process of transformation.

To conclude I should like to emphasize the nature of the new chemistry of radioactive bodies. Tons of material have to be treated in order to extract radium from the ore. The quantities of radium available in a laboratory are of the order of one milligram, or of a gram at the very most, this substance being worth 400,000 francs per gram. Very often material has been handled in which the presence of radium could not be detected by the balance, nor even by the spectroscope. And yet we have methods of measuring so perfect and so sensitive that we are able to know very exactly the small quantities of radium we are using. Radioactive analysis by electrometric methods allows us to calculate to within 1% a thousandth of a milligram of radium, and to detect the presence of $10^{-10}$ grams of radium diluted in a few grams of material. This method is the only one which could have led to the discovery of radium in view of the dilution of this substance in the ore. The sensitivity of the methods is still more striking in the case of radium emanation, which can be detected when the quantity present amounts, for example, to only $10^{-10}$ $mm^3$. As the specific activity of a substance is, in the case of analogous radiations, approximately in inverse proportion to the average life, the result is that if the average life is very brief, the radioactive reaction can attain an unprecedented sensitivity. We are also accustomed to deal currently in the laboratory with substances the presence of which is only shown to us by their radioactive properties but which nevertheless we can determine, dissolve, reprecipitate from their solutions and deposit electrolytically. This means that we have here an entirely separate kind of chemistry for which the current tool we use is the electrometer, not the balance, and which we might well call the chemistry of the imponderable.

# FREDERICK SODDY
## 1921

### INTRODUCTION

Frederick Soddy (September 2, 1877 – September 22, 1956) was an English radiochemist.

Soddy was born in Eastbourne, England. He went to school at Eastbourne College, before going on to study at University College of Wales at Aberystwyth and Oxford University (Merton College). He was a researcher at Oxford from 1898 to 1900.

In 1900 he became a demonstrator in chemistry at McGill University in Montreal, Quebec, Canada, where he worked with Ernest Rutherford on radioactivity. He and Rutherford realized that the anomalous behaviour of radioactive elements was due to the fact that they decayed into other elements. This decay also produced alpha, beta, and gamma radiation. When radioactivity was first discovered, no one was sure what the cause was. It needed careful work by Soddy and Rutherford to prove that atomic transmutation was in fact occurring.

His work and essays popularising the new understanding of radioactivity was the main inspiration for H G Wells's 1914 The World Set Free, which features atomic bombs dropped from biplanes in a war set many years in the future. Wells's novel is also known as The Last War and imagines a peaceful world emerging from the chaos. In Wealth, Virtual Wealth and Debt Soddy praises Wells's The World Set Free. He also says that radioactive processes probably power the stars. In 1903, with Sir William Ramsay, Soddy verified that the decay of radium produced helium.

From 1904 to 1914, he was a lecturer at the University of Glasgow and while there he showed that uranium decays to radium. It was here also that he showed that a radioactive element may have more than one atomic weight though the chemical properties are identical; this led to the concept of an isotope. Soddy later showed that non-radioactive elements also could have multiple isotopes. In addition he showed that an atom moves lower in atomic number by two places on alpha emission, higher by one place on beta emission. This was a fundamental step toward understanding the relationships among families of radioactive elements. Soddy published The Interpretation of Radium (1909) and Atomic Transmutation (1953).

In 1914 he was appointed to a chair at the University of Aberdeen, where he worked on research related to World War I. In 1919 he moved to Oxford University, where, in the period up till 1936, he reorganized the laboratories and the syllabus in chemistry. He received the 1921 Nobel Prize in chemistry for his research in radioactive decay and particularly for his formulation of the theory of isotopes. Frederick was also interested in technocracy and the social credit movement, which is evidenced by his publications Wealth, Virtual Wealth and Debt (George Allen & Unwin 1926) and Money versus Man (1933).

He died in Brighton, England.

## PRIZE ACCEPTANCE SPEECH

*Frederick Soddy's speech at the Nobel Banquet in Stockholm, December 10, 1922*

I wish to thank you for the very great honour which you have paid to my country, to the University of which I am a member, and to my students and myself, by the award of the Nobel Prize for Chemistry for 1921. In the first place, the preparation of the Nobel lecture which I am to give has shown me, even more clearly than I knew before, how many others share with me, often, indeed, have anticipated me, in the discoveries for which you have awarded me the prize. Secondly, I should like to recall that the two former British

Nobel laureates in Chemistry, Sir Ernest Rutherford and Sir William Ramsay were both my masters, and it is under them I received my training in scientific investigation. So that it is peculiarly gratifying to me to be chosen to receive the same honour as my distinguished teachers.

I take it almost as a personal compliment that Sweden so soon has donned her winter dress, for this work began for me with Rutherford in Canada, at Montreal, and the appearance of Stockholm today vividly recalls to me those early and exciting years. Ever since, I have felt that winter in the North speaks to the spirit of man with something of the appeal of Science. Nature is in austere mood, even terrifying, withal majestically beautiful. The pure air and dazzling snow belong to things beyond the reach of all personal feeling, almost beyond the reach of life. Yet such things are a part of our life, neither the least noble nor the most terrible.

It is appropriate, therefore, that this unique benefaction, which Science owes to Alfred Nobel, should be in the gift of Sweden and that Stockholm should be its home. Nowhere else, I am sure, in the whole world will one find, from the highest to the lowest, so eager a welcome for, or such universal appreciation of, the intellectual values that it was Nobel's desire to honour and advance.

The proposer of this toast has paid today generous tributes to the work of the new laureates, for which we all must feel, as I do, profoundly grateful. But he has touched also on the darker side of the picture. As a scientific man I wish to acknowledge and accept my own share of responsibility and blame for this. As scientific men we have all, no doubt, felt that our work has been put often to base uses, which must lead to disaster. But what sin is to the moralist and crime to the jurist so to the scientific man is ignorance. On our plane knowledge and ignorance are the immemorial adversaries.

Scientific men can hardly escape the charge of ignorance with regard to the precise effect of the impact of modern science upon the mode of living of the people and upon their civilisation. For them, such a charge is worse than that of crime.

The catastrophe which has recently engulfed the world has, however, not been without its own intellectual renaissance. The effects are not yet apparent, but, at least, perhaps not all of us are now totally blind to the dangers ahead, or to the need of that impersonal but remorseless re-examination of the foundations of society, which Science has already applied to the mechanism of the physical universe. Possibly it may fail. Perhaps it may be too late. Even so, yet I cherish the fancy that, whatever may happen in the crowded and fevered countries that are still ranged in fratricidal animosity, here at least, here in the Northlands, truth will endure.

# SIR ROBERT ROBINSON
## 1947

### INTRODUCTION

Sir Robert Robinson was born at Rufford, near Chesterfield, Derbyshire on September 13th, 1886, the son of William Bradbury Robinson, a surgical dressing manufacturer who invented his own machines for the production of lint, bandages, etc., and the cardboard boxes for packaging them. He was educated at the Chesterfield Grammar School, Fulneck School, near Leeds, and at Manchester University where he graduated B.Sc. in 1906 and D.Sc. in 1910.

In 1912, he was appointed the first Professor of Pure and Applied Organic Chemistry in the University of Sydney. He returned to Britain in 1915 to take the Chair in Organic Chemistry at the University of Liverpool until 1920 when he accepted an appointment as Director of Research at the British Dyestuffs Corporation. One year later, he became Professor of Chemistry at St. Andrews and in 1922 he took the Chair in Organic Chemistry at Manchester University until 1928 when he accepted a similar post in the University of London. In 1930, he was appointed Waynflete Professor of Chemistry, Oxford University, where he remained until his retirement in 1955 when he was appointed Emeritus Professor and Honorary Fellow of Magdalen College. He has been a Director of the Shell Chemical Company and a chemical consultant since 1955.

Sir Robert, a Fellow of the Royal Institute of Chemistry and of the Royal Society was President of The Chemical Society, 1939-

1941; of the Royal Society, 1945-1950; of the British Association for the Advancement of Science, 1955; and of the Society for the Chemical Industry, 1958. He is a Commandeur de la Légion d'Honneur and holds Honorary Doctorates of over twenty British and foreign universities. He has been honoured by The Chemical Society (Longstaff, Faraday and Flintoff Medals), the Royal Society (Davy, Royal and Copley Medals) and the Swiss, American, French and German Chemical Societies; he has also been awarded the Franklin Medal of the Franklin Institute of Philadelphia, the Albert Gold Medal of the Royal Society of Arts and the Medal of Freedom (U.S. Government). Sir Robert is Corresponding Member, Honorary Fellow, Foreign Member, Associate or Correspondant of almost fifty British and foreign learned societies.

In 1962, The Chemical Society honoured Sir Robert by establishing a Robert Robinson Lectureship, to be delivered biennially *in lieu* of the usual Presidential Address.

In 1912 Sir Robert married Gertrude Maud Walsh, a fellow student at Manchester University. They collaborated in several fields of chemical research, notably in a survey of anthocyanins. She died in 1954; they had one son and one daughter. In 1957, he married Stearn Sylvia Hillstrom (*née* Hershey) of New York.

In his younger days, Sir Robert was a keen mountaineer, having climbed in the Alps, Pyrenees, Norway and New Zealand, and he is an ardent chess player being President of the British Chess Federation, 1950-1953. His hobbies also include photography and music.

*Sir Robert Robinson died on February 8, 1975.*

## PRIZE ACCEPTANCE SPEECH

*Sir Robert Robinson's speech at the Nobel Banquet in Stockholm, December 10, 1947*

*Your Royal Highnesses, Your Excellencies, Ladies and Gentlemen,*

The winners of Nobel Prizes must be assumed to possess at least a modicum of imagination and sensibility and it is therefore incredible that any of us should not experience at this time a veritable surge of emotion. But it is hard to analyse our complex feelings and equally so to express them.

First we are all glad to have the opportunity of paying our sincere tribute to the memory of that great industrialist and philanthropist, Alfred Nobel, to whose generous impulse and high ideals we owe the possibility of these celebrations with all their ramifying consequences for the progress of culture in the broadest sense, and throughout the world.

Secondly, on behalf of all the foreigners here, I would wish to express our conviction that the noble traditions of the Swedish people, the physical framework of this beautiful city, and the whole intellectual atmosphere of your country, provide the unique medium in which the Nobel Foundation can grow and flourish. It is our hope and belief that Sweden herself derives great benefits from this conception of a genius who had the power to make his dreams come true.

For myself, I warmly thank the Nobel Foundation and the Committee for Chemistry for this mark of their approbation and for an award which confers the highest distinction that a scientist can achieve. I am greatly beholden also to my sponsors and supporters. It is well known that the Nobel Committees bring world opinion to a focus and that fact still further enhances the prestige attaching to the Prizes.

If I may now betray my own confidence I must confess that the news came to me as a pleasant surprise. I was much impressed by the perspicacity of the judges and jury. Not, I must hasten to say, that I disagree with their verdict! May I be allowed a few words to explain why their conclusion must have been difficult to reach. Of course I know that the summing up has already been provided by the eloquent partiality of Professor Fredga; I am most grateful for his kind words but am not absolved by them from making my own explanations. There is no one label that could be attached to me that would be thought adequate. I have never discovered a penicillin and I have not worked in the mines where ores of the more Nobeliferous metals are to be found. It has, however, been my privilege to have written a part of certain new chapters of organic chemistry. Such contributions as I have been able to make are to the science itself and do not derive their interest from the economic or biological importance of the substances studied. These are, as it were, analogous to the potters clay, or the sculptors stone, a kind of substrate for the exemplification of principles.

Finally, on behalf also of your guests, my wife and daughter, I thank you for the generous and thoughtful hospitality which we have experienced. We are indeed most grateful for the kindnesses showered upon us and we grasp with enthusiasm the hand of friendship extended to us.

# SIR CYRIL HINSHELWOOD
## 1956

### INTRODUCTION

Sir Cyril Norman Hinshelwood was born in London on June 19, 1897. He was educated at Westminster City School and Oxford University where he gained Master of Arts and Doctor of Science degrees. He held successive fellowships at Balliol, Trinity, and Exeter Colleges; he was tutor of Trinity College from 1921 to 1937 and since 1937 he has been Dr. Lee's Professor of Chemistry, University of Oxford. He is a delegate of the Clarendon Press and he has served as a member of several Advisory Councils on scientific matters to the British Government. He was elected Fellow of the Royal Society in 1929, serving as Foreign Secretary from 1950 to 1955, and as President from 1955 to 1960. He was knighted in 1948 and appointed to the Order of Merit in 1960.

His early studies of molecular kinetics led to the publication of *Thermodynamics for Students of Chemistry* and *The Kinetics of Chemical Change* in 1926, the latest (fourth) edition of the latter appearing in 1940, and he subsequently worked on chemical changes in the bacterial cell, producing physicochemical explanations for the biological responses of bacteria to changes in environment. His findings proved to be of great importance in later research work on antibiotics and therapeutic agents, and his book on the topic *The Chemical Kinetics of the Bacterial Cell* was published in 1946. He has contributed a great number of original papers and reviews to journals of learned societies and to other scientific periodicals, and his latest book, *The*

*Structure of Physical Chemistry* appeared in 1951.

Sir Cyril was President of the Chemical Society from 1946 to 1948, and President of the Faraday Society from 1961 to 1962, and included amongst the many awards he has gained are Lavoisier Medal, Société Chimique de France, 1935; Davy Medal, Royal Society, 1943; Royal Medal, 1947; Longstaff Medal, Chemical Society, 1948; Guldberg Medal, Oslo University, 1952; Faraday Medal, 1953; Avogadro Medal, Accademia dei Lincei, Rome, 1956; and Leverhulme Medal, Royal Society, 1960.

Honorary degrees conferred on Sir Cyril include Doctor of Civil Law (Oxford) and the Doctor of Science degrees of Bristol, Cambridge, Dublin, Hull, Leeds, London, Sheffield, Wales, and Ottawa Universities. He holds honorary memberships of the major scientific societies of many countries.

Sir Cyril is unmarried. He is fluent in many languages and his main hobbies are painting, collecting Chinese pottery, and foreign literature.

Sir Cyril Hinshelwood died on October 9, 1967.

## PRIZE ACCEPTANCE SPEECH

*Sir Cyril Hinshelwood's Address to the University Students on the Evening of December 10, 1956*

*May it please Your Majesties, Your Royal Highnesses, Students of Stockholm.*

Replying to this toast is a great responsibility for two reasons. On the one hand I have to speak for colleagues in a variety of different subjects and from various countries of the world. This consideration does not, however, weigh so very heavily on me. They have chosen me to speak for them, and therefore they must share the responsibility. Science and learning, moreover, are international, and just as earlier this evening I felt a special pleasure in the thought that Professer Semenov was representing me so now I hope we may all feel that a single spokesman is not inappropriate for what a great American called 'one world'. In learning at least that is true.

The responsibility which weighs rather more heavily on me is that in thanking the Students of Stockholm for their greeting, I am in a sense passing a message from an older to a younger generation. That is something which I feel all the laureates will regard as a matter of great moment, because I believe we have all been, and are, in one way and another teachers, and I believe most of my colleagues will feel, as I do, that the handing on of knowledge has been one of the most satisfying things in their lives.

What else can I say to you that none of my colleagues will want to contradict?

You are citizens of a great city, a great home of Swedish science, with illustrious names in every field, and at the same time, through the Nobel Foundation, a world capital in Science. We are confident that you will maintain the great traditions of your home city.

You see us today receiving great rewards. I think I can say that such things do not come by being sought. They are strokes of good fortune. Speaking for myself, I was surprised to receive the award. I expect most of my fortunate companions will support me when I say that to follow the urge to know is the chief reward which should be sought. And if good fortune comes it may be accepted with gratitude. Faraday once said that although he did not actually *want* to be proved wrong, he looked forward to the day when all he had written would by the advance of discovery come to belong to the bygone parts of science. Perhaps we should say that to you, and it will be for your generation to bring it about.

One last thing: I am speaking for representatives of Medicine, Physics, Chemistry and Literature. That we should stand together is an important symbol. You should remember that the division of knowledge into sciences and humanities is a false one. Both are parts of the great adventure of the human mind, and both should always be cultivated side by side. That is something which should never be forgotten.

Let me conclude by thanking you most sincerely for your greeting to us, and by offering with the warmest feelings of hope and confidence, our greeting to you: one generation to another.

# ROBERT B. WOODWARD
# 1965

## INTRODUCTION

Robert Burns Woodward was born in Boston on April 10th, 1917, the only child of Margaret Burns, a native of Glasgow, and Arthur Woodward, of English antecedents, who died in October, 1918, at the age of thirty-three.

Woodward was attracted to chemistry at a very early age, and indulged his taste for the science in private activities throughout the period of his primary and secondary education in the public schools of Quincy, a suburb of Boston. In 1933, he entered the Massachusetts Institute of Technology, from which he was excluded for inattention to formal studies at the end of the Fall term, 1934. The Institute authorities generously allowed him to re-enroll in the Fall term of 1935, and he took the degrees of Bachelor of Science in 1936 and Doctor of Philosophy in 1937. Since that time he has been associated with Harvard University, as Postdoctoral Fellow (1937-1938), Member of the Society of Fellows (1938-1940), Instructor in Chemistry (1941-1944), Assistant Professor (1944-1946), Associate Professor (1946-1950), Professor (1950-1953), Morris Loeb Professor of Chemistry (1953-1960), and Donner Professor of Science since 1960. In 1963 he assumed direction of the Woodward Research Institute at Basel. He was a member of the Corporation of the Massachusetts Institute of Technology (1966-1971), and he is a Member of the Board of Governors of the Weizmann Institute of Science.

Prof. Woodward holds more than twenty honorary degrees of which only a few are listed here: D.Sc. Wesleyan University, 1945; D. Sc. Harvard University, 1957; D. Sc. University of Cambridge (England), 1964; D. Sc. Brandeis University, 1965; D. Sc. Israel Institute of Technology (Haifa), 1966; D.Sc. University of Western Ontario (Canada), 1968;D.Sc. Universite de Louvain (Belgium), 1970.

Among the awards presented to him are the following: John Scott Medal (Franklin Institute and City of Philadelphia), 1945; Backeland Medal (North Jersey Section of the American Chemical Society), 1955; Davy Medal (Royal Society), 1959; Roger Adams Medal (American Chemical Society), 1961; Pius XI Gold Medal (Pontifical Academy of Sciences), 1969; National Medal of Science (United States of America), 1964; Willard Gibbs Medal (Chicago Section of the American Chemical Society), 1967; Lavoisier Medal (Societe Chimique de France), 1968; The Order of the Rising Sun, Second Class (His Majesty the Emperor of Japan), 1970; Hanbury Memorial Medal (The Pharmaccutical Society of Great Britain), 1970; Pierre Brnylants Medal (Université de Louvain), 1970.

Woodward married Irja Pullman in 1938, and Eudoxia Muller in 1946. He has three daughters: Siiri Anne (b. 1939), Jean Kirsten (b. 1944), and Crystal Elisabeth (b. 1947), and a son, Eric Richard Arthur (b. 1953).

*Robert B. Woodward died on July 8, 1979.*

## PRIZE ACCEPTANCE SPEECH

*Robert B. Woodward's speech at the Nobel Banquet in Stockholm, December 10, 1965*

*Your Majesty, Your Royal Highnesses, Ladies and Gentlemen.*

We are told that the Nobel festivities are a celebration of achievement. Therefore, I hope it will be regarded as appropriate for me to express my feeling that the things my fellow laureates and I have experienced here - the splendid and obviously so heart-felt hospitality, the magnificent ceremonies, and the unparalleled sense of occasion - all of these are in themselves achievements of the first rank. It is a high privilege for me to be a participant in this great occasion, and in many ways it cannot but be pleasant. But that pleasure is mixed with some concern, a concern which must have been shared by many, if not all, who have stood in this place. Can anyone deserve so concentrated an accolade? That concern for me is lessened if it is not suppressed by my awareness that my work has been done in close association with more than two hundred and fifty men and women. With them I have shared many challenges, surprises and pleasures, and their hands, their minds, and their hearts have brought me here tonight. And I am glad to have this opportunity to say in this very public place that they share this honor with me. But even this thought in a way gives rise to another concern. Alfred Nobel intended his prizes to be awarded for personal achievement. If I search for my personal achievement, it may be that I have led these men and women - and perhaps in some measure all organic chemists - to the higher ground of a greater appreciation of the power, and above all of the beauty of their science. If I have done this during the last almost thirty years, I have done it in circumstances which have been enormously exciting and quite rewarding enough in themselves. Beyond that, to have all this is somehow beyond one's dreams. For it, I thank you one and all.

# GERHARD HERZBERG
# 1971

## INTRODUCTION

Gerhard Herzberg was born in Hamburg, Germany, on 25 Dec., 1904. Herzberg received his early training in Hamburg and subsequ-ently studied physics at the Darmstadt Institute of Technology where in 1928 he obtained his Dr.Ing. degree under H. Rau (a pupil of W. Wien). From 1928 to 1930 he carried out post-doctorate work at the University of Göttingen under James Franck and Max Born and the University of Bristol. In 1930 he was appointed Privatdozent (lecturer) and senior assistant in the Physics Department of the Darmstadt Institute of Technology.

In August 1935 Herzberg was forced to leave Germany as a refugee and took up a guest professorship at the University of Saskatchewan (Saskatoon, Canada), for which funds had been made available by the Carnegie Foundation. From 1945 to 1948 Herzberg was professor of spectroscopy at the Yerkes Observatory of the University of Chicago. He returned to Canada in 1948 and was made Principal Research Officer and shortly afterwards Director of the Division of Physics at the National Research Council. In 1955, after the Division had been divided into one in pure and one in applied physics, Herzberg remained Director of the Division of Pure Physics, a position which he held until 1969 when he was appointed Distinguished Research Scientist in the recombined Division of Physics. Herzberg has been active as President or Vice President of several international commissions dealing with spectroscopy. He was also Vice President of the International Union of Pure and Applied Physics from 1957 to 1963. He held the offices of President of the Canadian Association of Physicists for the year 1956-57 and President of the Royal Society of Canada for the year 1966-67.

Herzberg was elected a Fellow of the Royal Society of Canada in 1939 and of the Royal Society of London in 1951. He was Bakerian Lecturer of the Royal Society of London in 1960 and received a Royal Medal from the Society in 1971. He was George Fischer Baker Non-Resident Lecturer in Chemistry at Cornell University in 1968, and Faraday Medallist and Lecturer of the Chemical Society of London in 1970. He is Honorary Member or Fellow of a number of scientific societies, including the American Academy of Arts and Sciences, the Optical Society of America and the Chemical Society. He is also a Foreign Associate of the National Academy of Sciences in Washington and a member of the Pontifical Academy of Sciences. He is a Companion of the Order of Canada. He has received many other medals and awards and holds Honorary Degrees from a number of universities in Canada and abroad, including one from the University of Stockholm.

*Gerhard Herzberg died on March 3, 1999.*

## PRIZE ACCEPTANCE SPEECH

*Gerhard Herzberg's speech at the Nobel Banquet in Stockholm, December 10, 1971*

*Your Royal Highnesses, Distinguished Guests, Ladies and Gentlemen,*

It is very difficult to find appropriate words to say "thank you" for an honour like the Nobel Prize. It is the supreme honour that a scientist can receive. Some of the giants in physics and chemistry have received this prize. Rutherford, the founder of nuclear physics, received the prize in chemistry in 1908. A number of those who have taught me either directly or indirectly are on that list: James Franck, Max Born, Peter Debye, Harold Urey and many others. I should also like to pay tribute to two pioneers in molecular spectroscopy from Sweden, Heurlinger and Hulthén, who accomplished the first difficult analyses of molecular spectra in the 1920's.

In receiving the award this year I think not only of these giants from whom I learned so much but also of my first teacher, Hans Rau, who guided my first steps in research, and to the many collaborators who helped me in my later work. Of them I should like to single out A. E. Douglas, whose quick and critical mind was always ready to help. I also think of my adopted country Canada, which gave a haven to me and my wife when we arrived as refugees. I think of the University of Saskatchewan which supported my work in its early stages and the National Research Council of Canada which provided an atmosphere so conducive to research.

Five years ago I received the great honour of an Honorary Degree from the University of Stockholm here in this building. It was at the same ceremony that His Majesty the King received an Honorary Degree from the Royal Caroline Medico-Chirurgical Institute. I felt doubly honoured that His Majesty was present throughout this ceremony. I could hardly have expected at that time that five years later I would stand here again in this building having received the great and supreme honour of the Nobel Prize from His Majesty's hands. I shall be forever grateful. Tack så mycket.

# WILLIAM LIPSCOMB
## 1976

### INTRODUCTION

WILLIAM N. LIPSCOMB was born on December 9, 1919 in Cleveland, Ohio, USA. William Lipscomb was educated at the University of Kentucky (BS 1941), Harvard University (MA 1959), Calfornia Institute of Technology (PhD 1946). He was Assistant Professor to Professor of Physical Chemistry at the University of Minnesota (1946-59) and Professor of Chemistry Harvard University (1971-). Guggenheim Fellowship Oxford (1954-55) and Cambridge (1972-73). NSF Senior Fellow (1965-66). Member of the National Academy of Sciences, Fellow of American Physical Society, American Chemical Society, American Academy of Arts and Sciences, Foreign Member of the Netherlands Academy of Arts and Sciences. Advisory Boards: Linus Pauling Institute of Science and Medicine, Dow Chemical Company, Robert A. Welch Foundation, Daltex Medical Science, Nova Pharmaceutical Corporation, Gensia Pharmaceuticals. Honorary Degrees: DSC University of Kentucky, Long Island University, Rutgers University, Gustavus Adolphus College, Marietta College, Miami University, University of Denver, Ohio State University. Nobel Prize in Chemistry (1976).

## PRIZE ACCEPTANCE SPEECH

*William Lipscomb's speech at the Nobel Banquet, December 10, 1976*

*Your Majesties, Your Royal Highnesses, Ladies and Gentlemen,*

The award this year of the Nobel Prize in chemistry for research in pure inorganic chemistry is an important event. It is a reminder that we know even now considerably less about most of the chemical elements than we know of the chemistry of carbon or the chemistry of processes underlying life itself. It is also a reminder that the inorganic area characterized by these other elements is now being incorporated into organic chemistry and biochemistry.

On this occasion in which intellectual achievement is given its highest recognition, those of us who are being honored should remind ourselves that we are tall only because we stand on the shoulders of others: those who have gone before us showing the way, those who worked with us as our colleagues, those who supported our research giving us funds, and those who have honored us, including you, most of all.

Finally, I take special recognition of the truly international nature of science. As a personal note, I take pleasure in recalling the remarkable association that I have had with many other research groups in different countries throughout the world.

# ELIAS JAMES COREY
# 1990

## INTRODUCTION

Elias James Corey (born July 12, 1928) is a renowned American organic chemist. In 1990 he won the Nobel Prize in Chemistry *"for his development of the theory and methodology of organic synthesis"*, specifically retrosynthetic analysis. Regarded by many as one of the greatest living chemists, he has developed numerous synthetic reagents, methodologies, and has advanced the science of organic synthesis considerably. He was awarded the Japan Prize in 1989.

He was born "William" to Christian Lebanese immigrants in Methuen, Massachusetts, 30 miles north of Boston. His mother changed his name to "Elias" to honor his father who died eighteen months after the birth of his son. His widowed mother, brother, two sisters and an aunt and uncle all lived together in a spacious house- struggling through the depression. He attended Catholic elementary school and Lawrence public High School.

At MIT, he earned both a bachelor's degree in 1948 and a Ph.D. in 1951. Both degrees were in chemistry. Immediately, he joined the faculty of University of Illinois at Urbana-Champaign. In 1959, he moved to Harvard University, where he is currently an emeritus professor of organic chemistry. He was awarded the American Chemical Society's greatest honor, the Priestley Medal, in 2004.

## PRIZE ACCEPTANCE SPEECH

*Elias J. Corey's speech at the Nobel Banquet, December 10, 1990*

*Your Majesties, Your Royal Highnesses, Ladies and Gentlemen,*

There is a children's poem by Julia Carney entitled "Little Things," one verse of which reads:

Little drops of water, little grains of sand
Make the mighty ocean and the pleasant land
Thus the little minutes, humble though they be
Make the mighty ages of eternity.

It is by countless small steps, like the little grains of sand, that we endeavor to understand ourselves and our universe, though confronted by endless complexity. Whatever our field - science, technology, humanities, art - we are excited by the challenge of research at an endless frontier, and also humbled by the vastness of our ignorance. We are heartened by the belief that knowledge, if wisely used, can benefit mankind.

My special fascination has been to understand better the world of chemistry and its complexities. Chemical compounds of carbon can exist in an infinite variety of compositions, forms and sizes. The naturally occurring organic substances are the basis of all life on earth, and their science at the molecular level defines a fundamental language of that life. The chemical synthesis of these naturally occurring substances and many millions of other carbon compounds has been one of the major enterprises of science in this century. That fact was affirmed by the award to me of the Nobel Prize in Chemistry for 1990 for the "development of the theory and methodology of organic synthesis." Chemical synthesis is uniquely positioned at the heart of chemistry, the central science. Its impact on our lives and society is all pervasive. For instance, most of today's medicines are synthetic and the majority of tomorrow's will be conceived and produced by synthetic chemists. To the field of synthetic chemistry belongs an array of responsibilities which are crucial for the future of mankind, not only with regard to the health and needs of our society, but also for the attainment of a deep understanding of matter, chemical change and life.

In the years after World War II, chemical syntheses were developed which could not have been anticipated in the earlier part of this century. For the first time, several complex molecules were assembled by elaborately conceived multistep processes, for example vitamin A, cortisone, morphine, penicillin, and chlorophyll. This striking leap forward was followed more recently by an equally dramatic advance in which chemical synthesis has been raised to a much higher level of sophistication. Today, in many laboratories around the world, chemists are synthesizing at an astonishing rate complex organic structures which could not have been made in the 1950's or 1960's. This advance has been propelled by the availability of new ways of thinking about chemical synthesis and the use of new chemical and physical methods. Many talented investigators all over the world have contributed to the latest surge of chemical synthesis. Their efforts constitute a collective undertaking of vast dimensions, even though made independently. Their ideas and discoveries interact synergistically to the benefit of all. I am happy to have been selected by the Nobel Committee for contributions to the science of chemical synthesis, but I am even more pleased that this important field of science has again received high recognition.

# GEORGE A. OLAH
## 1994

### INTRODUCTION

George Andrew Olah (born May 22, 1927, Budapest, Hungary, as *Oláh György*) is a Hungarian-born American chemist. He was significant in stabilizing and in studying carbocations via superacids. He won a Nobel Prize in Chemistry in 1994. Soon after, he was awarded the Priestley Medal, the highest honor granted by the American Chemical Society. Olah studied, then taught, at what is now Budapest University of Technology and Economics. As a result of the 1956 Hungarian Revolution, he and his family moved briefly to England and then to Canada where he joined Dow Chemical in Sarnia, Ontario. Olah's pioneering work on carbocations started during his eight years with Dow. In 1965 he returned to academia at Case Western Reserve University and then to University of Southern California in 1977. In 1971, Olah became a naturalized citizen of the United States. Olah is currently a distinguished professor at the University of Southern California and the director of the Loker Hydrocarbon Research Institute. In 2005, Olah wrote an essay promoting the methanol economy.

# PRIZE ACCEPTANCE SPEECH

*George A. Olah's speech at the Nobel Banquet, December 10, 1994*

*Your Majesties, Your Royal Highnesses, Ladies and Gentlemen,*

I am most grateful for the honor bestowed on me today. Although receiving the Nobel Prize is the greatest satisfaction any scientist can experience, I consider it not only a personal acknowledgment, but also that of all my students, associates and colleagues whose dedicated work over the years allowed my field of chemistry, which is not frequently highlighted in public, to be recognized.

There are many facets of chemistry. Mankind's drive to uncover the secrets of life's processes and use this knowledge led to spectacular advances in the biological and health sciences. Chemistry richly contributes to this by helping our understanding at the molecular level. Chemistry is, however, and always will be a central science of its own.

Chemists make compounds and strive to understand their reactions. My own interest lies in the chemistry of the compounds of the elements carbon and hydrogen, called hydrocarbons. These make up petroleum oil and natural gas and thus are in many ways essential for every day life. They generate energy and heat our houses, fuel our cars and airplanes and are raw materials for most manmade materials ranging from plastics to pharmaceuticals. Many of the chemical reactions essential to hydrocarbons are catalyzed by acids and proceed through positive ion intermediates, called carbocations.

To be able to prepare and study these elusive species in stable form acid billions of times stronger than concentrated sulfuric acid were needed (so called superacids). Some substituted carbocations, however, are remarkably stable and are even present in nature. You may be surprised to learn that the fine red wine we drank tonight contained carbocations which are responsible for the red color of this natural 12% or so alcoholic solution. I hope you enjoyed it as much as I did.

Chemistry does not always enjoy the best of reputation. Many of our plants and refineries are still potentially dangerous and may pollute their surroundings. At the same time our society enjoys a high standard of living not in small measure through the results of chemistry, which few would give up. I believe that chemistry can and will be able to bring about an equilibrium between mankind's needs and our environmental concerns. Chemistry will continue to benefit mankind in the spirit of Alfred Nobel, a fellow chemist whose example continues to inspire us all.

# AHMED ZEWAIL
## 1999

### INTRODUCTION

Ahmed Hassan Zewail was born on February 26, 1946 in Damanhur (60 km south-east of Alexandria). He is an Egyptian American scientist, and the winner of the 1999 Nobel Prize in Chemistry for his work on femtochemistry.

He received his first degree from the University of Alexandria before moving from Egypt to the United States to complete his PhD at the University of Pennsylvania with advisor Dr.Robin Hochstrasser. He completed a post doctorate at the University of California, Berkeley.

After some post doctorate work at UC-Berkeley, he was awarded a faculty appointment at Caltech in 1976, where he has remained since. He became a naturalized citizen of the United States in 1982, and in 1990, he was made the first *Linus Pauling Chair in Chemical Physics.*

Zewail's key work has been as the pioneer of femtochemistry—i.e. the study of chemical reactions across femtoseconds. In 1999, Zewail became the third ethnic Egyptian to receive the Nobel Prize, following Anwar Sadat (1978 in Peace) and Naguib Mahfouz (1988 in Literature). Other international awards include the Wolf Prize in Chemistry (1993) and the Robert A. Welch Award (1997). In 1999, he received Egypt's highest state honour, the Grand Collar of the Nile. Cambridge University awarded him an Honorary Doctorate in Science in 2006.

Zewail is married, and has four children.

## PRIZE ACCEPTANCE SPEECH

*Ahmed Zewail's speech at the Nobel Banquet, Dec. 10, 1999*

*Your Majesties, Excellencies, Ladies and Gentlemen,*

Let me begin with a reflection on a personal story, that of a voyage through time. The medal I received from his Majesty this evening was designed by Erik Lindberg in 1902 to represent Nature in the form of the Goddess Isis - or eesis - the Egyptian Goddess of Motherhood. She emerges from the clouds, holding a cornucopia in her arms and the veil which covers her cold and austere face is held up by the Genius of Science[1]. Indeed, it is the genius of science which pushed forward the race against time, from the beginning of astronomical calendars six millennia ago in the land of Isis to the femtosecond regime honored tonight for the ultimate achievement in the microcosmos. I began life and education in the same Land of Isis, Egypt, made the scientific unveiling in America, and tonight, I receive this honor in Sweden, with a Nobel Medal which takes me right back to the beginning. This internationalization by the Genius of Science is precisely what Mr. Nobel wished for more than a century ago.

In visionary words, Mr. Nobel summed up the purpose of the Prize: "The conquests of scientific research and its ever expanding field awake in us the hope that microbes - of the soul as well as of the body - will gradually be exterminated and that the only war humanity will wage in future will be war against these microbes". Mr. Nobel saw clearly what he wished for the world and the value of scientific discovery and advancement. Although there exist in the world today some microbes of the soul, such as discrimination and aggression, science was and still is the core of progress for humanity and the continuity of civilization. From the dawn of history, science has probed the universe of unknowns, searching for the uniting laws of nature. The world applauds your Majesties and the Swedish people for your appreciation, recognition, and celebration of discoveries of the unknown, which, according to Alfred Nobel will "leave the greatest benefit to mankind". I know of no other country that celebrates intellectual achievements with this class and passion.

To the world, the Nobel Prize has become the crowning honor for two reasons. For scientists, it recognizes their untiring efforts which lead to new fields of discovery, and places them in the annals of history with other notable scientists. For Science, the Prize inspires the people of the world about the importance and value of new discoveries, and in so doing science becomes better appreciated and supported by the public, and, hopefully, by governments. Both of these are noble causes and we thank you. To me, there is a third cause as well.

If the Nobel Prize had existed 6,000 years ago, when Egypt's civilization began, or even 2,000 years ago, when the famous library and university (museum) at Alexandria were established, Egypt would have scored very highly in many fields. In recent times, however, Egypt and the Arab World, which gave to Science Ibn-Sina (Avicenna), Ibn-Rushd (Averroës), Ibn-Hayan (Geber), Ibn-Haytham (Al Hazen), and others, have had no Prizes in science or medicine. I sincerely hope that this first one will inspire the young generations of developing countries with the knowledge that it is possible to contribute to world science and technology. As expressed eloquently in 1825 by Sir Humphrey Davy: "Fortunately, science, like that nature to which it belongs, is neither limited by time nor by space. It belongs to the world, and is of no country and of no age." There is a whole world outside the boundaries of the "West" and the "North" and we can all help to make it the microbe-free world of Mr. Nobel. I also hope that the Prize will help the region I came from to focus on the advancement of science, the Science Society, and on dignity and peace for humanity.

Your Majesties, I do not know how to express my own personal feelings and those of my family about this recognition. Behind this recognition, there exists a larger community of femtoscientists all over the world who tonight declare themselves proud. My own science family at Caltech of close to 150 young scientists represents the true army that marched to victory and made the contribution possible; they, too, must be proud of their effort. Personally, I have been enriched by my experiences in Egypt and America, and feel fortunate to have been endowed with a true passion for knowledge. I am grateful that this highest crowning honor comes at a young age when I can, hopefully, enjoy and witness its impact on science and humanity. The honor comes with great responsibilities and new challenges for the future, and I do hope to be able to continue the mission, recalling the thoughtful words of the great scholar, Dr. Taha Hussein:

ويل لطالب العلم إن رضى عن نفسه

which can be paraphrased in the following words: "The end will begin when seekers of knowledge become satisfied with their own achievements."

Thank you, Your Majesties. Thank you, all who are celebrating science and scientists.

# PETER AGRE
## 2003

### INTRODUCTION

Peter Agre (born January 30, 1949) is an American medical doctor and molecular biologist who was awarded the 2003 Nobel Prize in Chemistry (which he shared with Roderick MacKinnon) for his discovery of aquaporins. Aquaporins are water-channel proteins that move water molecules through the cell membrane.

Born in Northfield, Minnesota, he received his B.A. from Augsburg College in Minneapolis, Minnesota and his M.D. in 1974 from the Johns Hopkins University School of Medicine in Baltimore, Maryland. He currently serves as the Vice Chancellor for science and technology at Duke University Medical Center in Durham, NC, where he guides the development of Duke's biomedical research. He was elected to membership in the National Academy of Sciences in 2000 and to the American Academy of Arts and Sciences in 2003. He is also a founding member of Scientists and Engineers for America (SEA), and serves on its Board of Advisors.

Dr. Agre is known among science students for his humanity and humility. Perhaps this originates from the grade of "D" Agre received in his first chemistry class, despite having a father who was a chemistry professor.

He appeared on *The Colbert Report*, discussing SEA, sound science in politics, and the decline of American knowledge of science, among other topics.

Agre defended Thomas C. Butler, a plague researcher from Texas Tech University who voluntarily reported to the university safety office that 60 vials of plague bacteria were missing and had probably been autoclaved. Butler cooperated with FBI agents, who accused him of lying and arrested him. When Butler refused to plead guilty, federal prosecutors charged him with other charges, some of them unrelated, and he was convicted in a jury trial, lost his medical license, and served 2 years in prison.

In addition to being a founding member of Scientists and Engineers for Change, Agre was one of 48 Nobel aureates who signed a letter endorsing Massachusetts Sen. John Kerry for president.

Agre criticized many policies of the Bush Administration. "The Bush administration has been a disaster for the environment. They're playing Russian roulette by not signing the Kyoto Accord. If we wait until there's unequivocal proof that this is the cause of global climate change, it will be too late," he said.

On August 31, 2007, an editorial article written by Dr. Agre appeared in the Minneapolis Star Tribune.

Dr. Agre issued a call for a "...new century of science". In this editorial he highlighted the absolute paucity of scientists in Congress. He also contemplated the fact that both Germany and China have leaders who are trained research scientists (Germany: Angela Merkel, Ph.D., Physical Chemistry; China: Hu JinTao, Hydraulic Engineer).

There has never been a Nobel Science Prize winner in the U.S. Senate. Nor has there ever been a Nobel Prize winner elected Governor in the United States.

## PRIZE ACCEPTANCE SPEECH

*Peter Agre's speech at the Nobel Banquet, December 10, 2003.*

*Your Majesties, Your Royal Highnesses, Distinguished Guests:*

Written in 1895, Alfred Nobel's will endowed prizes for scientific research in chemistry, physics, and medicine. At that time, these fields were narrowly defined, and researchers were often classically trained in only one discipline. In the late 19th century, knowledge of science was not a requisite for success in other walks of life. Indeed, the 19th century painter James McNeil Whistler achieved artistic immortality despite failing chemistry at the U.S. Military Academy at West Point, an experience which he remembered with amusement, "Had silicon been a gas, I would have been a major general."

But the depth of science has increased dramatically, and Alfred Nobel would be astonished by the changes. Now in the 21st century, the boundaries separating chemistry, physics, and medicine have become blurred, and as happened during the Renaissance, scientists are following their curiosities even when they run beyond the formal limits of their training. This year a former physics student shares the Economics Prize, a philosophy student shares the Physics Prize, chemistry and mathematics students share the Medicine Prize, and medical students share the Chemistry Prize. Moreover, the subjects of this years prizes are linked. The discovery of superconduction, the Physics Prize, is the basis for magnetic resonance imaging, the Medicine Prize, that measures the distribution of water in tissues as governed by membrane channels, the Chemistry Prize.

The need for general scientific understanding by the public has never been larger, and the penalty for scientific illiteracy never harsher. In his masterpiece, *One Hundred Years of Solitude*, Gabriel García Márquez, winner of the 1982 Literature Prize, describes the isolated village of Macondo where the inhabitants suffer from their own naivete, trading their hard-earned gold for what they believe to be amazing inventions - a magnet, a magnifying glass, and even an enormous, transparent crystal that fascinated them being so cold it was painful to touch. What they regarded as the greatest invention of their time was only a block of ice.

In a way, the inhabitants of Macondo resemble contemporary individuals without any background in science. Lack of scientific fundamentals causes people to make foolish decisions about issues such as the toxicity of chemicals, the efficacy of medicines, the changes in the global climate. Our single greatest defense against scientific ignorance is education, and early in the life of every scientist, the child's first interest was sparked by a teacher.

Ladies and Gentlemen: please join Dr. MacKinnon and me in applauding the individuals that foster the scientific competence of our society and are the heroes behind past, present, and future Nobel Prizes - the men and women who teach science to children in our schools.

Tack så mycket.

# GERHARD ERTL
## 2007

### INTRODUCTION

Gerhard Ertl (born Oct. 10, 1936, in Stuttgart) is a German physicist and a Professor emeritus at the Department of Physical Chemistry, Fritz-Haber-Institut der Max-Planck-Gesellschaft in Berlin, Germany. He won the 2007 Nobel Prize in Chemistry. He completed his Diplom in Physics (equivalent to a Masters degree) at the Technical University of Stuttgart in 1961, followed his thesis advisor Heinz Gerischer from the Max Planck Institute for Metals Research in Stuttgart to Munich and received his PhD from the Technical University of Munich in 1965.

From 1968 to 1973, he was Professor and Director at Technical University of Hannover. Then, he became a Professor at Institute for Physical Chemistry, Ludwig Maximilians University of Munich (1973-1986). During the 1970s and 80s, he was also a Visiting Professor at the California Institute of Technology, the University of Wisconsin-Milwaukee and the University of California, Berkeley. He was director at the Fritz Haber Institute of the MPG from 1986 till his retirement in 2004. Ertl and his wife Barbara have two children and several grandchildren. His hobbies include playing the piano and also playing with his cats.

## PRIZE ACCEPTANCE SPEECH

*Gerhard Ertl's speech at the Nobel Banquet, 10 Dec. 2007*

The famous physicist Werner Heisenberg begins his autobiography with the sentence: "Science is made by men." Since in my own case you honour not a singular discovery, but the lifelong attempt to understand how chemical reactions at solid surfaces take place, this work involved in fact many people. When I was young, I was sometimes dreaming of becoming a musician. That is why I considered my co-workers often as an orchestra with me being the conductor. We know that even the best conductor cannot perform first class music with a mediocre orchestra. But I had the great luck of always being surrounded by an excellent group of co-workers whom I may compare – not with the Royal Stockholm Philharmonic Orchestra – but perhaps with the Berlin Philharmonic Orchestra. But in contrast to the situation with a real orchestra where the artists play notes prescribed by the composer, in our case the players themselves are the composers. By continuously crossing the border between the known and the unknown, they build on the never ending multidimensional symphony of science. The resulting feelings had once expressed by the greatest poet of my country, J. W. Goethe, when he was already over 80 years old: "Es geht nichts über die Freude, die uns des Studium der Natur gewährt" – "There is no greater joy than studying nature." Goethe died one year before Alfred Nobel was born, and hence he could not know that there might be an even greater joy, namely when ones own joy from studying nature is honoured in such a magnificent manner by the Nobel Prize.

*Thank you very much!*

# EI-ICHI NEGISHI
## 2010

### INTRODUCTION

Ei-ichi Negishi (born July 14, 1935) is a Japanese chemist who has spent most of his career at Purdue University, United States. He is best known for his discovery of the Negishi coupling. He was awarded the 2010 Nobel Prize in Chemistry "for palladium catalyzed cross couplings in organic synthesis" jointly with Richard F. Heck and Akira Suzuki. Negishi was born in Changchun, at that time the capital of Japanese-controlled Manchukuo, now the capital of Jilin, China. He graduated from the University of Tokyo in 1958, and did his internship at Teijin. He went to study in the United States and obtained his PhD from University of Pennsylvania in 1963 under the supervision of professor Allan R. Day. In 1966, He became a postdoc researcher at Purdue University, and became assistant professor in 1968, working with Nobel laureate Herbert C. Brown. In 1972, he went to become assistant professor at Syracuse University. In 1979, he was promoted to professor at Syracuse University. In the same year, he went back to Purdue University. In 2000 he was awarded the Royal Society of Chemistry's Sir Edward Frankland Prize Lectureship.

## PRIZE ACCEPTANCE SPEECH

*Ei-ichi Negishi's speech at the Nobel Banquet, 10 Dec. 2010*

Your Majesties, Your Royal Highnesses, Ladies and Gentlemen

I come humbly before you speaking for myself along with Co-Laureates - Dr. Richard Heck and Dr. Akira Suzuki. We are deeply honored to be recognized with this wonderful distinction. Receiving a Nobel Prize is the ultimate recognition for a lifetime spent questioning, exploring, experimenting; passing through the valleys of anguish to climb the mountains of success. For me, receiving this honor is a 50-year dream come true. I have known Dr. Heck and Dr. Suzuki for many years.

I have enormous respect and praise for their work in our field. I am particularly proud to say that both Dr. Suzuki and I did postdoctoral work at Purdue University with 1979 Chemistry Nobel Laureate Herbert C. Brown, who had a major influence on my life as well as my profession.

Our work in palladium-catalyzed cross-couplings in organic synthesis has been ongoing for many years and it will continue. But the full impact of it is not yet realized. Others will use what we have learned, build on what we have discovered and use this to help people and technology in ways that we can only imagine today.

The final reward for any researcher is to see his or her lifetime of work extend beyond academia and laboratories, into the mainstream of our global society where it can breathe hope into the world. Our pursuit in research must not be for rewards.

Our pursuit in whatever we do must always be for excellence, and if we accomplish excellence, it is its own reward and recognition will follow. This great honor inspires us to continue our quest for excellence.

Our gracious thanks to Your Majesties, the Nobel Foundation, the Nobel Committee for Chemistry, the Royal Swedish Academy of Sciences, our hosts who have so graciously escorted us through the excitement of these past several days, the people who have supported us and made this possible, and our families who share with us the joy of this moment.

Thank you.

# ROBERT J. LEFKOWITZ
# BRIAN K. KOBILKA
## 2012

### INTRODUCTION

Robert Joseph Lefkowitz (born April 15, 1943) is an American physician-scientist best known for his work with G protein-coupled receptors, for which, with Brian Kobilka, he was awarded the 2012 Nobel Prize for Chemistry. He is currently an Investigator with the Howard Hughes Medical Institute as well as a James B. Duke Professor of Medicine and Professor of Biochemistry and Chemistry at Duke University.

Lefkowitz was born on April 15, 1943, in The Bronx, New York to Jewish parents Max and Rose Lefkowitz. Their families had immigrated to the United States from Poland in the late 19th century.

After graduating from the Bronx High School of Science in 1959, he attended Columbia College from which he received a bachelor of arts in chemistry 1962.

He graduated from Columbia University College of Physicians and Surgeons in 1966 with an M.D. Degree. After serving an internship and one year of general medical residency at the College of Physicians and Surgeons, he served as Clinical and Research Associate at the National Institutes of Health from 1968 to 1970.

## INTRODUCTION

**Brian Kent Kobilka** (born May 30, 1955) is an American Nobel Prize winning professor in the departments of Molecular and Cellular Physiology at Stanford University School of Medicine. He is also the co-founder of ConfometRx, a biotechnology company focusing on G protein-coupled receptors. He was named a member of the National Academy of Sciences in 2011.

Kobilka, a Roman Catholic, attended St. Mary's Grade School in Little Falls, Minnesota, a part of the Roman Catholic Diocese of Saint Cloud.

He then Graduated from Little Falls High School. He received a Bachelor's Degree in Biology and Chemistry from the University of Minnesota Duluth, and earned his M.D., cum laude, from Yale University School of Medicine. Following the completion of his residency in internal medicine at Barnes-Jewish Hospital in St. Louis, Missouri), Kobilka worked in research as a postdoctoral fellow under Robert Lefkowitz at Duke University, where he started work on cloning the ß2-adrenergic receptor. Kobilka moved to Stanford in 1989. He was a Howard Hughes Medical Institute (HHMI) investigator from 1987-2003.

Kobilka is best known for his research on the structure and activity of G protein-coupled receptors (GPCRs); in particular, work from Kobilka's laboratory determined the molecular structure of the ß2-adrenergic receptor.[

This work has been highly cited by other scientists because GPCRs are important targets for pharmaceutical therapeutics, but notoriously difficult to work with in X-ray crystallography.

Before, rhodopsin was the only G-protein coupled receptor where the structure had been determined at high resolution. The ß2-adrenergic receptor structure was soon followed by the determination of the molecular structure of several other G-protein coupled receptors.

Kobilka is the 1994 recipient of the American Society for Pharmacology and Experimental Therapeutics John J. Abel Award in Pharmacology. His GPCR structure work was named "runner-up" for the 2007 "Breakthrough of the Year" award from Science.

The work was, in part, supported by Kobilka's 2004 Javits Neuroscience Investigator Award from the National Institute of Neurological Disorders and Stroke. He won the 2012 Nobel Prize in Chemistry with Robert Lefkowitz for his work on G protein-coupled receptors.

## PRIZE ACCEPTANCE SPEECH

*Robert J. Lefkowitz delivering his banquet speech.*

*Your majesties, your royal highnesses, your excellences, ladies and gentleman,*

To stand before this assembly as a Nobel Laureate in the midst of these gala and festive surroundings, is simultaneously daunting, exhilarating, empowering, and most of all humbling. It is a remarkable moment, one to be savored. It is also a moment in which to feel a profound sense of gratitude. And on behalf of Brian Kobilka and myself, I would like to extend our heartfelt thanks to the Nobel Foundation for making all of this possible, and to the Royal Swedish Academy of Sciences for selecting us as the 2012 Nobel Laureates in Chemistry. Our gratitude extends as well, to our collaborators and to the many dozens of students and fellows whose work in our laboratories is also honored by this award. We also thank our families, who are with us today for their unflagging support of our often obsessive involvement with our work, especially our wives Tong Sung Kobilka and Lynn Lefkowitz. Tong Sung is not just Brian's wife, but she has worked alongside him in the laboratory both as his technical assistant, dating back to his days in my laboratory more than 25 years ago, and for many years as his closest colleague and cheerleader, especially on his riskiest and most challenging projects.

No doubt, each Laureate's experience of receiving the Nobel

Prize is unique. For me, one of the most poignant aspects relates to sharing this award with a former fellow of mine. I don't know how often a Nobel Prize is shared by a mentor and former trainee, but perusing the list of recent winners suggests that it is a reasonably common occurrence. This highlights an aspect of science which is very important to both Brian and me, the mentoring of young trainees. I have trained more than 200 students and fellows in my lab over the past 40 years, and a number of mine and Brian's trainees have traveled to Stockholm to share this experience with us. They are in a very real sense a second family. Many of our trainees are major leaders in our field of science, a source of enormous pride for both of us.

But of course the annual award of the Nobel Prizes has significance that reaches far beyond the individual experiences of the Laureates. For those of us in the sciences, we watch with delight as every October the eyes of the entire world focus, if only transiently, on the power of discoveries in chemistry, physics, medicine, physiology, and economics to shape our lives.. However, as an American Scientist, and now Nobel Laureate, I have never been more aware or more appreciative of this effect of the Prize announcements. We have just had a Presidential election in the United States. One of the fault lines in the campaign was the role that science plays in shaping public policy decisions. A clear anti-science bias was apparent in many who sought the presidential nomination of one of our major political parties. This was manifest as a refusal to accept for example, the theory of evolution, the existence of global warming, much less of the role of humans in this process, the value of vaccines or of embryonic stem cell research. Each of us Laureates aspires in our own small way to do what we can to counter these pernicious anti-scientific trends.

The work for which Brian and I are recognized today is the elucidation of the largest class of cellular receptors. These are the molecules on cells with which hormones, neurotransmitters, and other biologically active molecules interact, and they are the commonest target of therapeutic drugs such as opiates, beta blockers, and antihistamines, to mention just a few.

Our work lies at the ever growing interface of chemistry and biology, a field generally referred to as biochemistry or biological chemistry, which is the Chemistry of living things. In this context, it is of note that Brian and I both began our careers as physicians, and have ultimately traveled a long road to ever more fundamental research, one which has now led us to the Nobel Prize in Chemistry. To me it seems very much the fulfillment of an aspiration so beautifully expressed in a line from a poem entitled Ithaca by the Greek poet Constantine Cafavy, which has been taped above my desk for many, many years. It reads, "When you set out on your journey to Ithaca, pray that the road is long, full of adventure, full of knowledge."

I can tell you this ... it certainly has been so far.

Brian and I thank all of you for celebrating this journey with us.

***Professor Sara Snogerup Linse delivering the Presentation Speech for the 2012 Nobel Prize in Chemistry at the Stockholm Concert Hall.***

*Your Majesties, Your Royal Highnesses, Ladies and Gentlemen,*

Like ingenious receivers, the G-protein-coupled receptors provide cells with sensibility. The receivers sense the composition of their surroundings. Based on what they find, different messages are delivered to the inside of the cell. Robert Lefkowitz and Brian Kobilka have shown us what these fantastic receptors look like, how they are built, how they function and how they are regulated in finest molecular detail. They have discovered that a whole family of receptors are built and act in a similar manner. Through evolution, these receptors have been refined to sense and distinguish almost a thousand signals. This lets us react to the adrenaline that rushes in our blood-stream when we get scared, the exciting scents and aromas that we will meet in the Blue Hall or the beautiful creations that already surround us. The joy we feel right now is indeed also due to G-protein-coupled receptors. The fluid surrounding our cells is filled with signalling substances. The receptors capture these and create euphoria in our cells.

Today we know the composition and function of many biomolecular systems, for example the ribosome - the protein factory of the cell. In addition, we know quite a bit about the driving forces that let molecules work together in time and space, so that complexes are formed fast enough and survive sufficiently long. But the number of possible combinations is almost infinite. In spite of this, or maybe thanks to this, evolution has given us a multitude of smart solutions for optimal cooperation. Also, because of this, it is difficult to predict what we have not yet observed. We may guess quite well, but still we miss many details and clever connections. When the discovery is there in front of us, with its intricate complexity revealed and simplified, we see and understand. We may even say: Of course! Oh yes! This is the way it must be! But we would never have guessed.

In the fairy-tale, the young dragon tells his friends that he wants to become a discoverer. "Discover what", one of his friends immediately asks. "Of course I cannot know beforehand", is the rapid and obvious response. In our own reality, scientists are often asked to tell beforehand what they are going to discover, preferably also by what method and sometimes also when the discovery will be made. Is it surprising that we sometimes wonder what is a fairy-tale and what is reality?

The ingenious creations of nature go far beyond our widest fantasy and imagination. This year's Nobel Prize in Chemistry is a brilliant example of this. When Robert Lefkowitz and Brian Kobilka entered the lab to investigate the beta-adrenergic receptor, they had no clue what would be revealed during the decades to come. They enjoyed the excitement over the unexpected finding of a family of structurally and functionally related receptors. Perhaps, they were as surprised as we to find that the receptors might be best called by another name.

Great discoveries often happen by serendipity, but by those who are observant and aware enough to reconsider their views. Such awareness stems from the experience and knowledge that arises when effort and time is spent to dig deep into the fundamentals of a scientific question. With great dedication, creativity and patience, Robert Lefkowitz and Brian Kobilka gradually learned to master the receptors. They developed methods to detect and lure them out of their shelters and to study them in almost every possible way. Over the decades they learned in the finest molecular detail how these receptors are built, how they transmit signals over the membrane and how they are regulated. The reward was extensive and rich. Their discoveries are molecular masterpieces in many respects. One of nature's wonders is now revealed in all its beauty. They have also given us a brilliant masterpiece in the form of powerful methodology and elegant strategies to study receptors of the greatest importance to mankind.

Brian Kobilka and Robert Lefkowitz. Your studies of G-protein-coupled receptors have revealed in the finest molecular detail an amazing signalling mechanism that lets our cells receive information from outside. That is a truly great achievement. On behalf of the Royal Swedish Academy of Sciences I wish to convey our warmest congratulations, and I now ask you to step forward and receive your Prize from the Hands of His Majesty the King.

~~~
~~~

# MAANU BEST SELLERS

₹ 125.00 Pages 208

₹ 125.00 Pages 208

₹ 125.00 Pages 208

₹ 250.00 Pages 512

₹ 160.00 Pages 192

₹ 145.00 Pages 200

₹ 160.00 Pages 224

₹ 125.00 Pages 112

₹ 135.00 Pages 192